THE MI

"What do you want me to do?" asked Seikei.

"Go to the monastery and make the emperor understand what his duties are."

Seikei stared. "But surely he must have advisers who have told him—"

"Of course he does," said the shogun, waving his hand. "They have clearly done a poor job of it. Now he distrusts them. But you . . . you will be able to persuade him."

Seikei doubted it, but he could see it was unwise to question the shogun's decision. The judge must have sensed Seikei's feelings, for he spoke up.

"He is fourteen," the judge said.

Seikei furrowed his brow. The shogun must know how old Seikei was.

"I mean the emperor," said the judge. "He is the same age as you are, and that is why the shogun feels you may be able to persuade him."

OTHER BOOKS YOU MAY ENJOY

The Boy Who Saved Baseball	John Ritter
The Demon in the Teahouse	Dorothy and Thomas Hoobler
The Ghost at the Tokaido Inn	Dorothy and Thomas Hoobler
Haunted	Judith St. George
The Hound of the Baskervilles	Sir Arthur Conan Doyle
In Darkness, Death	Dorothy and Thomas Hoobler
Shakespeare's Scribe	Gary Blackwood
Shakespeare's Spy	Gary Blackwood
The Shakespeare Stealer	Gary Blackwood
The Westing Game	Ellen Raskin

The Sword that Cut the Burning Grass

A SAMURAI MYSTERY

DOROTHY
&
THOMAS
HOOBLER

PUFFIN BOOKS
Published by the Penguin Group
Penguin Young Readers Group, 345 Hudson Street, New York, New York 10014, U.S.A.
Penguin Group (Canada), 90 Eglinton Avenue East, Suite 700, Toronto, Ontario, Canada M4P 2Y3
(a division of Pearson Penguin Canada Inc.)
Penguin Books Ltd, 80 Strand, London WC2R 0RL, England
Penguin Ireland, 25 St Stephen's Green, Dublin 2, Ireland (a division of Penguin Books Ltd)
Penguin Group (Australia), 250 Camberwell Road, Camberwell, Victoria 3124, Australia
(a division of Pearson Australia Group Pty Ltd)
Penguin Books India Pvt Ltd, 11 Community Centre, Panchsheel Park, New Delhi - 110 017, India
Penguin Group (NZ), Cnr Airborne and Rosedale Roads, Albany, Auckland 1310, New Zealand
(a division of Pearson New Zealand Ltd)
Penguin Books (South Africa) (Pty) Ltd, 24 Sturdee Avenue, Rosebank,
Johannesburg 2196, South Africa

Registered Offices: Penguin Books Ltd, 80 Strand, London WC2R 0RL, England

First published in the United States of America by Philomel Books,
a division of Penguin Young Readers Group, 2005
This Sleuth edition published by Puffin Books, a division of Penguin Young Readers Group, 2006

3 5 7 9 10 8 6 4 2

Designed by Gunta Alexander
Text set in New Baskerville

THE LIBRARY OF CONGRESS HAS CATALOGED THE PHILOMEL EDITION AS FOLLOWS:
Hoobler, Dorothy: The sword that cut the burning grass :
a samurai mystery / Dorothy and Thomas Hoobler.
p. cm.
Summary: In his latest adventure in eighteenth-century Japan, fourteen-year-old
samurai apprentice Seikei, with the help of a servant girl and an imperious old man,
sets out to rescue the young Emperor Yashuhito from his kidnappers.
1. Japan—History—Tokugawa period, 1600–1868—Juvenile fiction. [1. Japan—History—
Tokugawa period, 1600–1868—Fiction. 2. Kings, queens, rulers, etc.—Fiction. 3. Samurai—
Fiction. 4. Mystery and detective stories.] I. Hoobler, Thomas. II. Title.
PZ7.H76227Sw 2005 [Fic]—dc22 2004020320
ISBN 0-399-24272-4 (hc)

Puffin Books ISBN 978-0-14-240689-2

Printed in the United States of America

To Ellen

CONTENTS

The Sword that Cut the Burning Grass

Prologue

Yasuhito thought he could not sit still for another moment. The robes in which the priests had dressed him that morning were so heavy that he could not even stand up in them without help. They had had to lift him onto the throne, and then it took six priests to raise it onto a platform higher than the head of anyone in the hall.

Even there, Yasuhito could not rest. His arm ached from holding his sceptre upright as his officials approached, knelt, and then retreated on their knees. For most of the afternoon, the sickly sweet smell of incense had filled his nostrils. The sounds of chanting, gongs, flutes, and thirteen-string kotos *had gone on and on until he thought his head would burst.*

He saw with relief that the line of officials finally seemed to be coming to an end. Of course, Yasuhito knew, there might be still another group of them waiting outside the huge wooden doors of the Sacred Purple Hall. If he had had his way, he would have told them all to go home or do some work or what-

ever it was that they did when they weren't bowing in front of him.

But then he remembered the moment that morning when Uino, the high priest, had tied the ribbon that held Yasuhito's hat on.

Uino's face had been so close that Yasuhito could see the tiny red veins in his eyes and the hairs in his nose. Yasuhito was seldom frightened, because no one was permitted ever to hurt him, but Uino's eyes bored into his as if they were darts. Uino did not even have to speak, for Yasuhito knew what his message was: He had *to do this. Do it the proper way. The way he had been taught to do it for months, ever since his father had died. It was his duty.*

Yes.

And now, Uino approached again. At his signal, the younger priests lifted Yasuhito down from the high throne. With relief, he handed the sceptre to one of them. He stood quietly as they removed his outer garments and then the stiff, uncomfortable hat. Yasuhito raised his arms, just to experience the feeling, but immediately dropped them to his side again when he saw Uino's look of disapproval. No movements were permitted except those Yasuhito had rehearsed.

Uino pointed out the place where he was supposed to go now: a pool sunk into the floor at the far end of the hall. As Yasuhito reached the edge, another priest lifted the last of his clothing from his body, and Yasuhito stepped into the water. It was cool, soothing, and made him feel as if he weighed nothing at all. He imagined himself rising up to heaven, escaping all this . . .

Uino clapped his hands loudly. That got Yasuhito's attention, but it was the kami, *the spirits, that Uino was really calling. Uino began to chant a prayer. It was in the ancient language that people no longer spoke except here in the palace. He called on the kami to come and accept this boy, to let him be born again from Amaterasu, the goddess who had given birth to all his ancestors. The water would purify him so that he would be worthy. Yasuhito thought he saw Uino's eyes flick over him, as if he remembered how unworthy Yasuhito really was.*

Uino gestured again, and two priests ran forward carrying a long, rolled-up bamboo mat. They placed the beginning of it at the edge of the pool and started to lay it out in front of Yasuhito. Dripping and naked, he stepped onto it and began to follow as the mat unrolled. He knew that its purpose was to prevent his feet, now purified, from touching the floor. Another priest rolled the mat up behind him after he passed over it. No one but Yasuhito would be permitted to walk on the mat. No one but the emperor stepped here.

Yes.

He knew where they were going, where the unrolling mat would take him. He didn't really want to go there, but it was unthinkable to turn away, walk off the mat and go somewhere else.

What he wanted didn't matter. That was the strangest part about being the emperor.

Yasuhito followed the unrolling mat into a stone courtyard. The mat stopped at the entrance to a small wooden hut that appeared to be very old. The wood was full of wormholes and looked as if centuries of rain and wind had given it a moldy gray color.

Yasuhito knew that the hut had been built just this week. He had watched the carpenters from the window of his bedroom high above. They had used wood that was kept in a secret place. Tomorrow the hut would be taken down and put away until the next time a new emperor used it. Maybe that would be a long time, because Yasuhito was only eight years old.

A priest handed him the first of the three treasures: the sacred sword, the very one that Amaterasu's brother had taken from a dragon's tail. Yasuhito stepped off the end of the carpet and went inside the hut. Candles were burning all around the walls, and he could see a low table in the center of the room. Two bowls of rice sat on the table, steaming as if they had just been placed there. Between them lay the other two sacred treasures: the jewel and the mirror. All three treasures had been gifts from Amaterasu herself, presented to one of Yasuhito's ancestors thousands of years before. They had been passed down to each new emperor ever since.

A pillow covered with silk rested on the floor, and he sat down, relieved that he could be comfortable at last. No one would disturb him until the next morning. No one else could come inside, except of course the goddess herself. Amaterasu would enter the hut during the night. When she appeared, Yasuhito would be reborn, just as all his ancestors had been when they became the emperor.

That worried him a bit. "Does it hurt?" Yasuhito had asked Uino, which made Uino angrier than Yasuhito had ever seen him.

"Do you remember being born before?" asked Uino.

Yasuhito admitted that he did not.

"Then it didn't hurt," said Uino, "and even if it does, you will never speak of it to anyone."

One *person would know if it hurt or not. Grandfather would know. But he was gone now. Yasuhito had last seen him four years ago, when Father became the emperor. Yasuhito had overheard some of the servants say that Grandfather had gone to live on the summit of Fujiyama, where he spoke only with the spirits of nature.*

Amaterasu would know how to find Grandfather, Yasuhito told himself. She knew everything, because day and night she watched over all of Japan. He had many questions to ask her. She would tell him what he wanted to know. All he had to do was wait for her to arrive.

Yes.

1 — A Strange Task

"I have a task for you," said the *shogun.*

Seikei found himself unable to speak. The shogun wanted *him* to do something? He glanced at his father Judge Ooka, who was seated to the shogun's right. A third man, dressed in a *kimono* with a hollyhock design that identified him as a shogunate official, sat on the other side of the shogun. They were in a room that was usually used for much larger meetings. Reflecting the shogun's simple tastes, the walls were bare and the only furniture, aside from straw mats and pillows, was a small table that held a teapot and some porcelain cups.

The judge smiled to break the silence and said, "Perhaps Seikei feels unworthy of serving you."

"Oh, *no!*" Seikei blurted out. "I mean, yes, I'm unworthy, but no, I'll do anything you want."

The shogun nodded. "Your father told me when he wanted to adopt you that you have the true *samurai* spirit. He was correct. You haven't even asked what the task will be. Suppose I wanted you to defend me against a *ninja* who was determined to kill me?"

"I would," Seikei said instantly.

"He has already defeated a ninja," murmured the judge.

"That's right," said the shogun. "He does not lack for bravery." He gave Seikei a look of approval and pride. It warmed Seikei's heart until he noticed the expression on the face of the third man. His dark brown eyes were as hard as flint stones, and showed his clear contempt. Seikei, who was always conscious that he had not been born into a samurai family, felt that the man must know Seikei's original father had been a lowly merchant.

"You would not need weapons for this task," the shogun continued. Seikei could not prevent his hand from reaching to touch the hilt of his long sword. He had only recently earned the right to carry it by defeating the ninja. He would have fought to the death to keep it. The twin swords at his waist—one long, one short—were the mark of a samurai warrior.

The shogun noticed his gesture. "No need to defend me here," he said dryly.

Seikei felt his face grow hot. They were inside the shogun's castle in the heart of Edo. There was likely no safer place in all Japan. Indeed, just to draw one's sword from its scabbard here carried a penalty of death.

The shogun poured another cup of tea for the judge, who was one of his most trusted officials and friends, and a cup for the other man as well. Seikei nodded politely when the Shogun looked in his direction, and saw his cup filled too. It was the highest quality tea, as Seikei well knew, for his original father had been a seller of tea.

As his guests sipped the thick, greenish liquid, the shogun said, "What I tell you must remain a secret, for it could cause alarm if others learned of it."

Seikei nodded. Japan had been at peace for more than a century, ever since the shogun's ancestor, Tokugawa Ieyasu, defeated the last of the warlords who had fought among themselves for control of the country. It was the shogun's responsibility to maintain the peace so that harmony would reign and everyone could prosper.

The shogun leaned forward, as if intending that his words would reach Seikei alone. The walls of the room were made of decorated paper in light bamboo frames, and even a trusted servant might be listening. "The emperor has fled from his duties."

Seikei blinked. The emperor? He had heard of the emperor, of course. Supposedly he lived in a great palace in the city of Kyoto, far to the west, on the other side of

Lake Biwa. Seikei's first father, the tea merchant, had occasionally visited Kyoto on business. He once told Seikei, "The emperor is a kami, a divine spirit, and as with other kami, you cannot see him."

"Does that mean he isn't real?" Seikei had asked. He had been very young then.

"Of course he's real," Father had scolded. "Don't we visit shrines to call on the kami for assistance? Do you think we would do that if they weren't real? And look—they've helped me gain wealth by selling tea. Now if only I could find a kami to put some sense into your head and stop you from wanting to be a samurai instead of a merchant."

Seikei realized that the shogun was waiting for him to respond. "Ummm . . . well, I'm sure the judge can find the emperor, wherever he may be." Everyone knew that the judge could solve any mystery, find any criminal, determine the truth in any case brought before him. Seikei had on a few occasions helped him, but only by doing what the judge had told him to.

The shogun nodded. "The truth is," he said, "we already know where the emperor is." He turned to the third man, who took it as a command to speak.

"He did not even leave Kyoto," the man said. "He fled to a monastery, the Kinkakuji, the Golden Pavilion. The monks will protect him for now. A very trustworthy person is looking after him."

Seikei thought he saw the problem. "And the monastery is a sacred place, so the emperor cannot be taken from it?" The last time he had helped the judge solve a case, some Shinto priests had sheltered a ninja who had committed a crime. The judge had to get their permission for Seikei to go after him.

But no. The third man curled his lips, making Seikei feel even stupider. The shogun explained, "No one may lay his hands upon the emperor. He cannot be forced to do anything."

"Well," said Seikei, "if he is safe there . . . why not leave him there?"

The shogun sighed. "If only that were possible. The problem is that he doesn't want to be the emperor."

"He doesn't?" Seikei was so surprised, he almost laughed. But he caught himself, because he could see from the shogun's face that this was a serious matter. "But . . . he can't *stop* being the emperor."

The shogun frowned. "He can stop performing the emperor's duties."

"What are those like?" Seikei asked warily.

The shogun looked at Judge Ooka. "Perhaps you can explain this better than I can," he said.

"If you were a farmer," the judge said to Seikei, "you would understand this more quickly."

Seikei hung his head, embarrassed that he wasn't understanding quickly enough.

"The emperor's ancestor is the goddess Amaterasu," the judge said. "She has always loved and protected Japan. Each year, part of the emperor's duty is to ask her for good weather and fertile soil so that there will be an abundant harvest. In the winter, then, there will be plenty of rice and no one will go hungry." He patted his large round stomach. "As you know, I dislike going hungry, so it is important to me as well."

"It's not amusing," growled the shogun. "The emperor is supposed to make a public appearance at the time of the spring solstice. He must plow a furrow of land and plant rice seeds. If he doesn't perform that duty, word will spread, and the farmers will be afraid to plant their own seeds. At harvesttime, they will not deliver the proper amount of rice to their *daimyo* lords. The daimyos will bring this problem to me. They will say they are unable to pay their taxes." He looked sternly at Seikei, making him feel that somehow it would be *his* fault. "This must not be allowed to happen," the shogun said, raising his voice.

"What do you want me to do?" asked Seikei.

"Go to the monastery and make the emperor understand what his duties are."

Seikei stared. "But surely he must have advisers who have told him—"

"Of course he does," said the shogun, waving his hand. "They have clearly done a poor job of it. Now he distrusts them. But you . . . you will be able to persuade him."

Seikei doubted it, but he could see it was unwise to question the shogun's decision. The judge must have sensed Seikei's feelings, for he spoke up.

"He is fourteen," the judge said.

Seikei furrowed his brow. The shogun must know how old Seikei was.

"I mean the emperor," said the judge. "He is the same age as you are, and that is why the shogun feels you may be able to persuade him."

2 —
The Judge's Warning

When they left the palace, the judge explained, "I suggested the idea to the shogun, and he agreed. He is very anxious to find a solution to this problem."

He must be desperate, Seikei thought silently, to think that the emperor would listen to what *I* have to say. A groom brought their horses and helped the judge to mount his. The palace grounds were immense, and at this time of year, the views were breathtaking. Swirls of red and yellow leaves ran through the treetops, contrasting with the dark green of pines and cedars. Seikei and the judge rode slowly, enjoying the spectacle.

"What does he look like?" Seikei asked. He tried to imagine himself talking to a kami, and he kept thinking of an old tree with huge, twisted limbs behind the tea shop in Osaka. Everyone believed that a very powerful kami lived within it, and Seikei often sat there and prayed that it would find a way for him to become a samurai. The kami had granted his request, but he doubted that the emperor looked like a tree.

"The emperor? I have not seen him myself," said the judge. "But I am told he is not very different from any other boy. He became emperor when he was only eight years old, but he performed all his duties correctly until recently. The chief priest, a man named Uino, died suddenly this year. Perhaps the emperor was affected by his death."

"I suppose his father is dead too, or he wouldn't be the emperor."

"Yes, his father is," replied the judge. Something in his voice made Seikei think there was more to the story. He looked questioningly at the judge.

His foster father smiled. "You are alert, I see," he said. "The emperor's grandfather is still alive. He was the emperor at one time, but retired, thinking that it was time his son had the responsibility. Unfortunately, the son did not live to an old age, and *his* son took the throne."

"Well, why doesn't the shogun ask the grandfather to become the emperor again? That would solve everything."

"Unfortunately, once one has relinquished the power of the *Tenno Haike,* one cannot assume it again. Amaterasu would not permit it. Besides, no one knows where the grandfather is. Unlike his grandson, he has successfully hidden himself."

"And the emperor's mother?" Seikei would have done anything to please his own mother, but he knew she would never ask anything of him.

"She is dead too," said the judge, "and the emperor was her only child."

"It sounds as if no one wants to be the emperor," said Seikei. "Why is that?"

"That's something you may discover for yourself," replied the judge. "Being emperor is a heavy responsibility. Perhaps some would find the burden unbearable."

"Duty is an honor that Heaven bestows on us," Seikei said.

The judge smiled. "I have read that too," he said.

"Well, isn't it true?" asked Seikei.

"Many things are true," replied the judge. "It is also true that not all people agree on what is true."

This was so confusing that Seikei had no answer. The sound of approaching hoofbeats behind them made him turn his head. The official who had been present at the meeting with the shogun rode by swiftly. He shot Seikei another of his scowls.

"Who was that man?" Seikei asked the judge after he was out of earshot.

"He is Yabuta Sukehachi, the chief of the Guards of the Inner Garden."

"I have never heard of them before," said Seikei.

"With good reason," said the judge. "It is a crime just to mention that they exist."

Seikei didn't know how to respond. It seemed to him that the judge must have just confessed to a crime, but that was unthinkable.

"As you see," the judge said after a moment, "even I sometimes fail in my duty. In this case, my concern for your safety overcame my devotion to the law of the shogun."

"My safety? Do you think I am in danger?" Seikei asked. He stared at the back of the rapidly receding horse and rider ahead of them.

The judge saw where he was looking. "It is Yabuta's job—his duty, really—to bring information to the shogun. It was he who found where the emperor was, and he wanted the shogun to assign him the task of bringing the emperor back to the palace."

"Why didn't he?"

"Because Yabuta would have done it by force."

"But if there is no other way to persuade the emperor to perform his duties . . ." Seikei trailed off.

The judge reined his horse to a halt. They were overlooking a particularly beautiful spot in the palace grounds. A breeze was plucking some of the autumn-colored leaves from the trees. For a moment, he and Seikei enjoyed the scene, and then the judge spoke: "Did you ever hear the story people tell about the three great military leaders who unified our country? Someone brought them a songbird that would not sing. Nobunaga said, 'I will order it to sing.' Hideyoshi declared, 'I will kill it if it doesn't sing.' But Tokugawa Ieyasu, the shogun's ancestor, said, 'I will wait until it decides to sing.' " He turned to Seikei. "That is why the shogun would prefer not to use Yabuta for this task."

The judge rode on, and Seikei followed, thinking about what he had said. By the time he started to reply, they had reached the gate in the wall surrounding the palace grounds. Several samurai guards were standing there, and the judge gestured for Seikei to be silent.

When they had passed through and into the street beyond, the judge said, "From now on, you must be careful about where you speak and what you say. Yabuta was insulted that you were chosen for a task he believed he should carry out. He will report to the shogun anything he can find that reflects badly on you. Some people say he has eyes that he can leave in rooms that will let him see what goes on there."

"Do you believe that?"

The judge shrugged. "I think it very likely that he employs servants and guards to tell him things they see and hear. So consider your actions carefully when you are in Kyoto."

"I would never do anything to dishonor our family," said Seikei.

"No, not intentionally. But an innocent act or remark may be misunderstood. When I judge cases that are brought before me, I do not like information that has passed through too many mouths."

"It would be better if *you* had the ability to leave your eye anywhere," said Seikei.

To one side of the street, some acrobats stood on one another's shoulders to form a pyramid. The judge stopped his horse to watch, and Seikei did likewise.

"I would not like to have that ability," said the judge.

For a second, Seikei thought he was talking about the acrobats. Then he realized the judge meant the ability to see anywhere. "But you would be able to make everyone safe," Seikei protested.

The judge shook his head. By now, the pyramid numbered ten men, starting with four on the bottom row. It was quite impressive. "They would not be safe from *me*," said the judge. "I am only a man, not perfect. I might use that ability to make myself more powerful. I would be tempted to use it against people I did not like. Who knows what effect it might have on me?"

The acrobat on the top of the pyramid jumped down, and the crowd watching the performance gasped. It seemed as if he would be badly hurt, but at the last moment, two of the men on the bottom of the pyramid reached out and caught him. The crowd cheered. The acrobats began to hold out cups for a donation. The judge handed over a silver coin that was accepted with a smile and a bow.

As they rode on, Seikei took the conversation in another direction. "Does that mean," he asked, "that you would not like to be the emperor?"

"Indeed I would not," replied the judge. "He has responsibility but no power. The shogun is the ruler of Japan for most things. The emperor is more important, because he is our link with Heaven, but I do not feel that would be a comfortable role for me."

"Then how am I going to convince him to perform his duties?" asked Seikei.

"I am sure you will think of something," said the judge.

"Will you be there to advise me?" Seikei did not have the same confidence in his ability as the judge did.

"Unfortunately, I have duties that will prevent me from traveling with you," said the judge. "The fire brigades that we have established throughout Edo need additional training. For the same reason, I cannot spare Bunzo to go with you. You will be on your own."

Seikei nodded. Bunzo was the chief of the judge's samurai forces. After the judge had adopted Seikei, Bunzo had trained him in the skills a samurai should have. Seikei was keenly aware that he had not always measured up to Bunzo's standards. Still, it would have been reassuring to have him along on this trip. Seikei knew that Bunzo would, if necessary, give his life to defend him.

"It should take you six days to reach Kyoto," said the judge. "I suggest you start tomorrow morning."

Seikei recalled the last time he had traveled along the Tokaido Road. It was a journey that had changed his life. He felt a little uneasy about having to start out again, as if tracing his steps in the other direction might be bad luck, might take him back to the life he had led before.

3
The Ronin's Complaint

Traveling, Seikei soon found, was a different experience from what it had been when he was a tea merchant's son. Before, when he and his old father encountered a great daimyo lord on the road, they had to move aside and bow humbly until the procession of samurai warriors and servants of the daimyo had passed by. This could cause long delays, for some daimyos traveled with as many as a thousand retainers.

Now, since Seikei's *haori* jacket bore the shogun's crest, he had to move aside for no one. The sign of the hollyhock was known and respected everywhere. When Seikei stopped at an inn, he did not have to give "thank-money" to the innkeeper to ensure that his room would be comfortable. As soon as he dismounted, a groom took his horse. At the door, a servant brought him a hot towel and asked if he wished tea. By the second day of his journey, Seikei was sending the tea back if it was not of high quality. The servants were surprised that he could tell good tea from bad.

The following day, he asked to be served a particular kind of fish that he knew was a specialty of the local area. He imagined it was expensive, but he had already learned that he would not receive a bill at the end of his stay. The innkeepers sent any bills to the shogun, and hoped they would be paid.

The weather made the trip even better. Every day was clear and crisp, the chilly air seeming to bring added color to the autumn leaves still clinging to the trees. When Seikei passed Mount Fuji, he could see its snow-covered summit clearly. Only a few years before, the volcano had erupted, sending streams of molten lava down its sides, but now it stood once more in silent, frosty majesty, linking the land with Heaven.

That set Seikei thinking about his task. He supposed the emperor must be a very strange person, something like the hermits who were supposed to live high up on Mount Fuji. They did nothing but meditate, and survived by drinking melted snow and eating berries and pinecone nuts. Seikei thought it might be possible that the emperor was so concerned with spiritual matters that he didn't consider his earthly duties important. Perhaps it would help to tell him of the many people who would go hungry if the rice crop was poor. But maybe he would be meditating so deeply that he wouldn't notice Seikei at all. What then? Seikei would not like to go back to the shogun and admit that he had failed.

The road was crowded here at the base of Mount Fuji, for at this time of year many people came to view the sacred mountain. Seikei became so deeply engrossed in thought that he failed to notice a samurai approaching from behind on foot. Suddenly the man tugged at the leg of Seikei's *monohiki,* which he wore for riding.

Seikei looked down and instinctively reached for his sword. The man wore two swords himself, as well as a plain brown *kosode* that was stained and fraying a bit at the end of the sleeves. He evidently was a *ronin,* one of the masterless samurai who wandered about, searching for a daimyo to take them into his household.

When the ronin saw Seikei touch the hilt of his sword, he dropped to his knees in front of the horse. "Forgive me, Your Honor," he said. "I saw from your clothing that you were a courier for the shogun. I have an urgent message for him. I must tell him of a great injustice."

Seikei reined in his horse. It was either do that or ride over the man. Some passing workmen, carrying tools to advertise their trades, momentarily stopped to stare. "Get up!" Seikei told the man in a low tone. "Act like a samurai!"

Slowly the man rose to his feet, but kept his head bowed.

"I am on a mission for the shogun," Seikei told him. "It will take me to Kyoto. Why don't you report this injustice to the local governor?"

The man looked up, his eyes white with fear. "Oh no, Your Honor," he said. "The officials here would do nothing."

Seikei looked at the man's shabby condition. "When was the last time you ate?" he asked.

The man shook his head. "I had some pears yesterday. They fell off a farmer's cart. I did not steal them. I swear it."

"There was a woman selling noodles back on the road a little way," Seikei said. He handed the man a coin. "Go and get yourself a bowl."

"But you haven't heard my report," the man protested.

"If you write it out," Seikei said, "you can give it to any of the shogun's couriers heading for Edo." He pointed in the direction he had come from. "That way," he said. "But I'm going to *Kyoto*."

The man hung his head again. "Alas, Your Honor, I am ashamed to say I cannot write." Slowly he looked up, peering hopefully at Seikei. "But you could write it for me."

Seikei sighed.

The man actually ate *three* bowls of noodles, and would no doubt have consumed even more had Seikei not figured out that the more he ate, the longer his story became. It was a confusing tale, hardly believable. The ronin's name was Takanori, and he had been born into a samurai family that served a daimyo named Lord Shima.

Lord Shima's domain had not been large, but somehow he had aroused jealousy in a more powerful neighbor, Lord Ponzu. Over many years, it seemed, Lord Ponzu had brought ruin to his neighboring daimyo. He and his samurai had tormented the farmers who worked in Lord Shima's fields—diverting streams to cause floods, letting rats loose in granaries, killing farm animals in the night. . . . There seemed to be no end to Lord Ponzu's despicable tricks.

Seikei tried to hurry the story along. "Didn't Lord Shima resist?"

"What could he do?"

"Complain to the local magistrate," Seikei said.

Takanori shook his head. "Whenever my lord brought a complaint, the magistrate would look the other way. And indeed, Lord Ponzu acted in such secrecy that nothing could be proven."

Seikei said nothing. Judge Ooka had told him that such things happened. The reason the shogun had promoted the judge to high office was because of the judge's honesty, which unfortunately was a rare quality.

"Well, what happened?" Seikei asked. "Clearly you are no longer employed by Lord Shima."

"My lord grew desperate," said Takanori. "One day, he encountered Lord Ponzu on the road between their domains. Lord Ponzu dared to insult him. My lord was compelled to draw his sword to defend his honor, and Lord Ponzu's men cut him down, along with all the samurai with him. Two of my lord's personal guards were my brothers, and they died that day."

Seikei said nothing. His opinion was that Takanori, to save his own honor, should have fought and died as well. Now look at him! Little more than a beggar. The two swords he wore were the only indication that he had once been a samurai. Seikei had heard that some people like Takanori, because of poverty, had even sold their swords to go into business. He turned away in disgust.

"Your story has merit," Seikei said, "but as I told you, I cannot return to Edo just now. I have—"

He stopped, shocked, because Takanori had taken hold of his arm and pulled him close. He could smell the green onions from the soup the man had eaten. "There's more," Takanori said. "When I tell you this, you'll see how important it is that the shogun be told."

Seikei angrily pulled away. "Be quick with it, then," he said. "But no more soup."

Takanori looked around, as if he feared someone was listening. Not even the woman selling soup looked as if she cared in the slightest about what he had to say.

"Lord Ponzu is planning an uprising against the shogun," he whispered.

At first Seikei was stunned, but almost immediately a wave of anger rolled over him. This was a transparent lie, intended to trick Seikei into thinking he had to go back to Edo at once.

"How do you know this?" he asked coldly. "Have you any proof?"

"I . . . I heard it from a *geisha* who said two of Lord Ponzu's men spoke of it while drunk. But she is very reliable. If the shogun sent someone to investigate—where are you going?"

Seikei had gotten to his feet and headed for the door

of the noodle shop. He stopped only to say, "I am sorry for the misfortune that you have encountered. I will report your story to an honest magistrate, but not until I have finished my work in Kyoto." He turned his back and ignored the man's feeble protests.

4 — Porridge with the Emperor

On the remainder of his trip to Kyoto, Seikei had trouble getting the incident out of his mind. Even the sight of Lake Biwa, the vast blue body of water just east of the imperial city, could not erase it. Of course the ronin's story was concocted to bring attention to whatever injustice might have been done to his daimyo master. But suppose there was indeed some kind of plot to overthrow the shogun? Then clearly Seikei ought to report it at once.

No. The shogun would have laughed at the story—until he remembered that Seikei had shirked his duty to carry out the task entrusted to him.

Seikei felt a sense of relief when he reached Nijo Castle, the governor's residence in Kyoto. The servants there treated him as if he were an important person. Of course, Seikei decided after thinking about it, since he was on an official mission, he *was* an important person.

After Seikei had been served excellent tea and a meal of fresh fish with rice, he was invited to meet the governor. He changed into a formal kosode for the meeting. The shogun's representative in Kyoto turned out to be a short, middle-aged man who continually brushed away wrinkles in his kimono. "I am informed that you are to receive any assistance I can provide," he told Seikei. "I understand you plan to speak personally with the emperor."

"As soon as that can be arranged," Seikei responded.

"This is most unusual," said the governor. "Normally, not even *I* would speak to the emperor. When I have anything to communicate to him, I send a message to the Minister of the Right at the imperial palace." He tugged at one of the sleeves of his kimono, then smoothed it with his finger. "Or the Minister of the Left," he added.

"Is the emperor still at the Golden Pavilion monastery?" asked Seikei.

"Yes. I have ordered the monks to inform me if he should try to leave."

Seikei smiled to himself. He knew that monks of important temples followed the "orders" of government officials only if it suited them. "Could you assign someone to show me the way to the pavilion?" he asked.

"Perhaps tomorrow afternoon?" suggested the governor. "Or is that too soon?"

"I would like to go now," said Seikei.

The governor was so surprised that he smoothed both of his sleeves. Evidently things did not get done as quickly in Kyoto as they did in Edo. "Right now?" the governor asked.

"If that can be arranged," said Seikei.

It could. Accompanied by a mounted samurai named Kushi, Seikei rode to the northern part of the city. At the foot of a high hill stood a gate surrounded by two stone pillars. "That is the entrance," Kushi said. "Leave your horse here and walk up the path to the temple."

"Aren't you coming?" asked Seikei.

"It will be better if I don't," said Kushi. "The monks here follow the Zen form of Buddhism. One moment they seem to be meditating, and the next they're testing their military skills. If I were you, I would leave my swords behind so that no one challenges you."

Seikei hesitated. "I cannot give up my swords without good reason."

Kushi shrugged. "As you like. Will your errand take some time?"

"I don't know," admitted Seikei.

Kushi indicated a *sake* shop on the other side of the street. "I'll wait there for you," he said.

The monastery gate was open and unguarded. Seikei walked up the narrow stone path beyond it and entered a grove of trees. In places, grass and weeds had sprouted between the stones underneath Seikei's feet. He was surprised no one had tended to them.

The path followed the base of the hill until suddenly it reached a clearing. Seikei saw a massive three-tiered pagoda with overhanging roofs that gleamed gold in the midafternoon sunlight. The sight was breathtaking until he looked a bit closer. Like the path, the pagoda seemed a bit shabby. Railings on the upper floors were broken, and a few of the roof tiles were missing or out of place.

No one appeared until Seikei reached the pagoda. Then a monk in an orange robe emerged from a doorway. He looked strong and carried a device that consisted of two iron bars held together at one end by a grip. Seikei recognized it as a *jitte.* Practicing with Bunzo, he had seen a man with a jitte trap a warrior's sword and wrench it from his grasp.

"What is your purpose here?" called the monk.

"I have come to speak to the emperor," Seikei replied.

"We do not use titles here," the monk told him.

Seikei thought back to what he'd learned. "Then I

wish to speak to Yasuhito," he said, using the emperor's personal name, even though it was supposed to be unlucky to do so.

"He is meditating," said the monk. "His teacher may not allow you to disturb their session."

"I will respect that," said Seikei. "I can wait."

The monk looked at Seikei's swords. "No one may bring weapons into our sanctuary," he said.

Seikei sighed. Kushi had been right. It would have been better to leave his swords outside. Since had had no desire to challenge this monk, who was probably highly skilled, Seikei would have to surrender them here.

He untied the scabbards from his *obi* and held them out. The monk stepped back and indicated a wooden sword rack on the porch. As Seikei placed his weapons there, he noticed that some other visitor had left a set as well.

Seikei walked in the direction the monk pointed out. As he rounded the side of the pagoda, he beheld a scene of such beauty that he stopped to stare at it. Chrysanthemums, hundreds of them, bloomed in the sunlight as if someone had spread bronze and yellow blankets over the ground. In the midst of this blaze of color was a blue pond with oddly shaped gray rocks jutting from its surface. One of the larger rocks, split in two, had two pine trees growing from it. Beyond the pond was a forest of trees, some evergreen, others in full fall splendor, which created the illusion that the Golden Pavilion was in a remote wilderness, instead of the heart of a busy city.

Two monks, one young, one old, sat on a wooden platform overlooking the pond. Seikei was sorry to disturb them, for he could imagine how pleasurable it was to rest here. In fact, he thought, he himself would find the natural beauty of the spot too distracting for meditation.

As Seikei set foot on the platform, the older monk looked up. He got to his feet and walked toward Seikei. The monk's eyes seemed much younger than the rest of him, they seemed to take in everything about Seikei at a glance. "I see you have come from the shogun," the monk said. He had noticed the design on Seikei's kosode.

"Yes," said Seikei. "He sent me to talk to the em—to Yasuhito. Is that him?"

Instead of answering, the monk turned to look at the pond and said, "The scent of chrysanthemums."

At first Seikei thought he was commenting on the view. Then he realized that the phrase was the beginning of a well-known poem. " 'And in Nara,' " Seikei quoted, " 'All the ancient Buddhas.' "

The monk gave Seikei a second look, one of reappraisal. Seikei could tell that the poem had been a test and that the monk had not expected him to pass it. The monk could not have known that Basho, the samurai who had written those lines, was Seikei's favorite poet. As a tea merchant's son, Seikei had not been able to practice the samurai skills of swordsmanship or archery. But he could read poetry (and even try to write some himself, as samurai did), and Basho had become his inspiration. Now he recalled that Basho had adopted Zen Buddhism, so it shouldn't have been surprising that his poems had become aids to meditation.

The monk stood aside as if to invite Seikei to join the emperor. Seikei approached warily. If anything, the emperor looked younger than fourteen. The expression on his face was far from peaceful. He looked annoyed, as if something about the scene made him want to wade out and correct the placement of the rocks in the lake, uproot some of the flowers, or remove a tree or two.

Seikei sat down an arm's length away from him, trying to make as little noise as possible.

"You've interrupted my meditation," said the boy, without looking away from the pond.

"I'm sorry," said Seikei.

"It doesn't matter. I'm no good at it anyway." The boy

finally glanced at Seikei. "Would you like some porridge?" he asked.

"No."

"I would. That's all I could think about while I was meditating." He motioned for the older monk to come closer. "Oyuka, bring me some *ginkgo*-nut porridge. And a bowl for him too," he said with a nod in Seikei's direction.

Wordlessly, the monk departed. Seikei felt a little embarrassed by the way the boy had treated the older man.

"I really don't want porridge," said Seikei.

"I heard you the first time," replied the boy. "If Oyuka brings two bowls, I can have twice as much. They'll give me anything I ask for, but they try to get me to eat less, so the bowls will be small."

Seikei nodded. "Why do they do that?"

"They think it's better for me spiritually to eat less. There are shrimp in the porridge, and the Buddhists don't approve of eating animals."

"Actually," said Seikei, "I meant to ask, why do they bring you anything you ask for?"

The boy started to answer, but stopped. He eyed Seikei coldly. "What's your name?" he asked.

"I am Seikei, son of Ooka Tadesuke, samurai and official of the shogun," Seikei said formally.

"Hah!" the boy responded with a smirk. "Very proud of it, aren't you?"

Seikei took a moment to calm himself, for he didn't want to begin by pushing the emperor into the pond. "Yes," he said. "I am proud of who I am. And who are you?"

"Oyuka calls me Risu, Squirrel, because I like ginkgo nuts so much."

"Is that who you are, then? A squirrel?"

A flicker of annoyance replaced the boy's mocking look. Then it disappeared. "I have a lot of names. Risu is as good as the others."

Oyuka returned with a tray that held two steaming bowls of soup. After setting them down, he waited for more instructions. "Go away," Risu told him. "I feel like talking to Seikei some more. He amuses me."

The porridge smelled good, rich and nutty. As Risu sipped from his bowl, Seikei reached for the second one. He hand was slapped away before he could touch it.

"You didn't want any, remember?" said Risu.

Seikei's face felt hot. He saw now that it had been a good idea to leave his swords behind. After he had calmed down, he said, "Some people say that if the emperor strikes them, they will die."

"Sounds stupid to me," commented Risu between

sips. "I've struck lots of people and only a few of them died, and those not right away." Risu suddenly thought about what he'd said. He put his bowl down on the tray, a bit too hard, making a clatter. Risu glared at Seikei, and then picked up the second bowl as if daring him to object.

"So you are the emperor?" Seikei asked quietly.

"People *think* I am," admitted Risu. "But they're wrong."

5 — THE MINISTERS DO NOT AGREE

True, Seikei thought to himself, Risu did not fit his idea of what the emperor would be like. But he had never met an emperor before, so perhaps his idea was incorrect.

"Why would people think you are the emperor, if you aren't?" Seikei asked him.

Risu shrugged. "Who knows? They need to believe that someone is the emperor. I was only a child, and they chose me."

"Didn't you . . . like being the emperor?"

"You don't hear things well, do you? I already told you I'm not the emperor."

"Yes, but I mean, didn't you like the things you have to do if . . . people *think* you're the emperor? Like planting rice seeds in the spring. You've done that before, haven't you?"

Risu looked around as if wondering where Oyuka had

gone. Seikei could tell he didn't find the conversation so amusing now. Seikei had to find a way to get Risu's attention.

"If you don't plant those seeds this year, they won't bring you that ginkgo porridge any more," said Seikei. "What will you do then?"

Risu's eyes narrowed as he looked at Seikei. "Oyuka will still—" he began, then said, "I'll become a monk. That's what I'm here to do."

"Do all the monks eat that porridge? Or just you?"

Risu did not answer.

"Look," said Seikei. "Why don't you just plant the rice seeds again this spring? I don't know if you'd be such a good monk. You know, everyone has a place in life . . . a duty to fulfill, and yours—"

"How can you say that?" interrupted Risu. He seemed truly upset. "I'm supposed to act like the emperor even if I know I'm *not*? Why don't *you* pretend you're the emperor and plant the seeds?"

I wish I could, thought Seikei. "Well, in the first place," he said, "people know I'm not the emperor. What made you think you weren't? You *did* plant the rice seeds before, didn't you?"

"Yes," Risu said, very quietly.

"Did you think you weren't the emperor then?"

"I wasn't sure," Risu replied. "Anyway, Uino made me do it. He was the high priest, but he's dead now. He could make you do anything."

"Is that why you decided you weren't the emperor? Because he died?"

"No, no," Risu said, waving his hands. "When I became emperor and was waiting for Amaterasu . . . well, I'm not going to tell you about *that.* But this year, after Uino died, I read a scroll in the palace library, and I learned why . . . why . . . " He wasn't sure how to finish.

"Why you weren't the emperor?" Seikei prompted.

"Why Amaterasu didn't come to *see* me!" Risu said. He was angrier than ever, almost on the point of tears.

Seikei was confused, but he felt as if he'd found out something important. "Where is this scroll now?" he asked.

Risu had turned his back. "Go away," he said. "I'm meditating."

"Look, just tell me—" Seikei stopped because he felt a hand on his shoulder. He looked up to see that Oyuka had appeared out of nowhere.

"Perhaps you could return some other time," the monk said. His voice was calm, but something about it made Seikei feel he had to obey.

Seikei got to his feet. He looked down at Risu, trying to think of something else he could say.

Risu sensed that he hadn't left. "It's the Kusanagi scroll," he said over his shoulder. "But *you'd* never understand it."

Seikei didn't need Oyuka to escort him out. He walked up the path to the pagoda, stopping there for a last look at the scene. This time, he noticed another person seated in a meditative position across the pond. His hair was white, and he was wearing a dark blue kimono. Seikei supposed he must be the person who had left the other set of swords on the porch of the pagoda. He was probably there just to meditate, but the thought crossed Seikei's mind that he might have overheard his conversation with Risu. If so, it didn't seem to have broken the man's concentration.

Across the street from the temple, Kushi was still waiting for Seikei. "I have to go to the imperial palace," Seikei told him.

The samurai snorted. He seemed to have had a few cups of sake in the meantime. "You're wasting your time," he told Seikei, "if you expect to accomplish anything there."

"Why do you think so?"

"I've been there before on errands for the governor. The emperor has two chief ministers—one of the Right, one of the Left. You have to obtain the consent of both of them just to deliver a message to the emperor."

"What's so difficult about that?" Seikei asked.

"The two ministers never agree. That's their function. The idea is to give the emperor more than one opinion, but now it stops him from hearing anything at all, so he never has to make a decision."

Evidently Kushi didn't know the emperor was no longer in the palace. "I'll try anyway," Seikei said. "My request is a simple one."

But nothing, he found, was simple where the Ministers of the Right and Left were concerned. They sat side by side on two raised platforms in a hall larger than the one the shogun used for major official meetings. Both ministers were dressed alike—in crimson kimonos decorated with the imperial chrysanthemum. The gatekeeper who brought Seikei into the room instructed him to sit on a mat in front of the two ministers and wait for one to speak.

Both were reading scrolls and sipping tea. They paid no attention whatsoever to Seikei. If he had been treated this way in any other place, Seikei would have taken it as a great insult to the shogun. Since in theory the emperor was superior to the shogun, Seikei knew that this was only a demonstration of the ministers' high rank.

At last the Minister of the Right—or at least the one who sat on the right, from their point of view—rolled up his scroll and acted as if he had noticed Seikei for the first time. Instead of addressing him, however, he turned to the other minister.

"Are you occupied?" he asked.

"I'm quite busy," the Minister of the Left replied.

"Shall I handle this task myself?" the Right one asked.

The Left one lowered his scroll and glared at Seikei. The hollyhock design on Seikei's jacket seemed to influence his response. "No. It might be important," he said, adding, "and you might make a mistake."

"State your business," the first minister said to Seikei.

"I wish to read a scroll in the palace library," said Seikei.

"No," the Minister of the Left responded at once.

"I disagree," said the other minister. "We should at least find out what scroll he wishes to read."

"The Kusanagi scroll," said Seikei.

"No," replied the Minister of the Right. Seikei's heart sank.

"Your request is an interesting one," said the Minister of the Left, raising Seikei's hopes again. "How did you learn of the Kusanagi scroll?"

Seikei took a deep breath. He thought of something the judge had once said: "Unless it is obvious that revealing the truth will cause harm, it is always better to tell the truth than to lie. For to lie is to begin creating a world that does not exist, and then you must create the rest of that false world too."

"The emperor told me about it," Seikei said.

The effect of this was startling. Neither of the two ministers seemed to be able to reply. First they stared at Seikei, and then at each other. One of them picked up his scroll again, as if thinking to find an answer there. The other took a writing brush from his sleeve, but did nothing except wave it in the air.

Finally the Minister of the Right recovered enough to ask, "Did . . . did the emperor indicate why he was interested in that scroll?"

Seikei considered this.

"Not that this scroll has any *real* interest," said the Minister of the Left.

Seikei decided that again, the truth was best. "He said it would help me understand why he isn't the emperor," said Seikei.

"Out of the question," the Minister of the Right said firmly.

"You could *have* the scroll, but we might not be able to find it," said the other minister.

"But if we *could* find it, you wouldn't be able to read it," said the other one.

"And if you could read it, you wouldn't *understand* it," added the first one.

"Even if you understood it—" the other one continued.

"He wouldn't," the first one interrupted.

"But if he *did*," said the second one.

"Stop it!" Seikei shouted. His voice sent echoes around the vast hall.

They stared at him.

"You're not allowed to shout in here," the Minister of the Right said.

"Unless you have good reason," his colleague added.

"But you don't," said the first minister.

Seikei replied before the other minister could. "Yes, I do. I am on official business for the shogun, and on his authority I request to see the scroll. I can bring samurai to enforce his orders, if necessary."

"Oh, the shogun," the Minister of the Right said in a mocking voice.

"The emperor is superior to the shogun," the Minister of the Left informed Seikei.

"In all things," said the other minister. Together, they gave Seikei smug looks. On this point, apparently, they were not going to contradict each other.

Seikei felt angry. "The emperor is not here," he said. "What if *he* orders you to show me the scroll?" Seikei knew this was highly unlikely, but he wanted to jolt the ministers out of their feelings of superiority.

He didn't succeed. "The emperor is young," said the Minister of the Right.

"Young people," said the second one with a meaningful look at Seikei, "need guidance."

"He may not be able to exercise good judgment," said the first minister. "That is why we are here to advise him."

"Or he *may* exercise good judgment," pointed out the second one.

"In either case, *we* will decide."

"If we agree."

And of course, thought Seikei, the two ministers would never agree on anything.

6 — Death Visits the Monastery

Seikei left the palace with a feeling of helplessness. Very likely the governor would not go so far as to send samurai to compel the ministers to give up the scroll. And Seikei's threat to ask the emperor to issue an order was an empty one. Who could tell if the emperor would even speak to him again?

Kushi showed him the way back to the governor's residence. There, Seikei was given a guesthouse separate from the main building. He could order anything he liked for his evening meal, but failure had robbed him of hunger. After picking at a tray of tea and plain rice, he sat trying to think of a plan until sleep overcame him.

When he awakened, someone was rapping at his door. Annoyed, he wanted to ignore it until he heard Kushi's voice. When Seikei slid the door open, he saw not only Kushi but two other samurai. The looks on their faces were considerably less friendly than the ones Seikei had encountered yesterday. "Get dressed," Kushi said. It was not a request. "The governor wants to see you immediately." No one asked if Seikei would like tea.

Neither did the governor. He was finding many wrinkles in his clothing this morning, and the look he gave Seikei seemed to suggest who was to blame.

"There has been an unfortunate development," said the governor.

Seikei had guessed that much.

"The emperor has disappeared again."

Seikei blinked. He would not have guessed *that.* "I thought the monks were guarding him."

"Yes, the monks." The governor pulled fiercely at one of his sleeves. "Some of them were killed."

Killed? "How did this happen?"

"You do not know?"

"How could I know? Have you sent a magistrate to investigate? My father Judge Ooka—"

The governor's angry look cut him off. "I am aware of your *foster* father's reputation. However, another of the shogun's officials is already investigating the case. He is at the monastery. My men will take you there." The governor smoothed out a few more of the distracting wrinkles. "My advice," he told Seikei, "is to tell him the truth, because he will have you tortured if you don't."

Seikei could do nothing but stare.

On the way to the monastery, Seikei realized that the three samurai were there to keep him from fleeing. But how could the governor think *he* had anything to do with these new events?

Once more they left their horses at the monastery gate. This time, at least six other horses were tethered there as well. Seikei wanted to study the path inside to look for traces that intruders might have left, but the samurai hustled him forward.

At the pagoda, several monks were at work. Two were washing the wooden steps, while others burned incense and chanted. Seikei understood clearly that a violent death had occurred here. No doubt the heavyset monk with the jitte had been overcome, at the cost of his life. Here too, Seikei tried to stop to examine the scene, but his guards would not permit it.

As they rounded the side of the pagoda, Seikei beheld the same scene that had appeared so beautiful yesterday. Now, death had blighted it. Some of the chrysanthemums at the edge of the pond had been trampled and broken. Samurai who had not left their swords behind were searching the banks, and it was true: The presence of their weapons disrupted the serenity of the garden.

Two of the samurai were standing over what first appeared to be a bundle of wet cloth. As Seikei came closer, he realized it was the body of a monk they had apparently pulled from the lake. Even more disturbing, at least to Seikei, was the appearance of someone he had not expected to meet here in Kyoto.

Walking toward Seikei was Yabuta Sukehachi, the chief of the Guards of the Inner Garden—the very person Judge Ooka had warned Seikei not to come afoul of. The look on Yabuta's face indicated he was not about to congratulate Seikei on his success at persuading the emperor to resume his duties.

"You were here yesterday," said Yabuta, just stating a fact. Seikei nodded.

"I want you to look at something," Yabuta said. He led Seikei to the body that had been pulled from the water. One of the samurai standing there turned it over on its back. "Do you recognize him?" asked Yabuta.

Seikei almost turned away. The eyes were open and the teeth still clenched in anger, even though a gash across his neck had drained the blood from the face.

"It's Oyuka, the monk who was teaching Ri—I mean, the emperor, to meditate."

"Did you think he was dangerous?" The tone of Yabuta's voice put Seikei on guard.

"This man? No, he wasn't dangerous at all."

"Would it surprise you to learn he was probably the most skilled person in the monastery at the art of *jujutsu*?"

Jujutsu? The art of combat without using weapons? Seikei had seen a demonstration of it by the ninja Tatsuno, who had brought down a horse and an armed warrior with only his hands. "I saw no indication of that," said Seikei.

"How many people do you think it would have taken to overpower him?"

"He was old. Anyone might have overpowered him," said Seikei, but he recalled the aura of authority that the monk had exuded.

"Five men could not have overpowered him," Yabuta said firmly. "Unless it was a person he was told to protect and not touch." Yabuta looked at Seikei. "Or someone who could approach him while concealing a knife and arouse no suspicion."

Who could Yabuta be referring to? Seikei asked himself. The emperor? But why would—?

Yabuta snapped out a question. "What did you say to the emperor yesterday?"

Seikei tried to remember. It had been a confusing conversation.

Yabuta took his hesitation as weakness. "You were supposed to persuade him to resume his duties," he reminded Seikei. "Did you?"

"Well . . . he said he wasn't the emperor."

"But of course you saw through that." Now Yabuta was being sarcastic. "Let's see if we can improve your memory." He signaled to one of the samurai, and Seikei turned to see the Ministers of the Right and Left being led down the hill from the pagoda. They looked indignant, like two peacocks who have had their feathers ruffled by a hawk.

As they drew closer, one of them recognized Seikei and pointed. "That's the one!" he called out. Yabuta smiled with satisfaction. The other minister glared suspiciously at Seikei, but remained silent.

"You have seen this samurai before?" Yabuta asked the minister who had spoken.

"He came to the palace yesterday," the minister replied.

"Yesterday *afternoon*," the second one added.

"He threatened us," the first one said.

"Ordered, *then* threatened," corrected the second one.

Yabuta broke in. "Ordered you?" he asked. "Ordered you to do what?"

"To give him a scroll from the palace library."

"Acted as if he could *understand* it."

"Said he would get the emperor to *command* us to give it to him."

"Said he would—"

Yabuta cut off the conversation with a flick of his hand. He turned to Seikei. "Why did you ask for this scroll?"

"The emperor . . . ," Seikei began.

"I thought you said he *wasn't* the emperor," Yabuta said.

"*He* said he wasn't the emperor." Seikei was aware that he was being made to sound foolish.

"Go ahead," said Yabuta. "What was on this scroll?"

"I don't know," Seikei admitted. "The emperor—the boy who was here yesterday—said that the scroll would explain why he wasn't the emperor."

Both of the ministers drew back in horror. "*Not* the emperor?" one of them cried in a shrill voice. "That's nonsense."

"Sacrilege," added the second. He turned to Yabuta. "You should execute him for insulting the emperor."

"I will decide what action to take," said Yabuta firmly.

He looked at Seikei and in a silky voice said, "Tell me, what did the emperor say when you returned here?"

"When I returned? I did not return," said Seikei.

"No? You told these ministers that you would obtain an order from the emperor, didn't you?"

"I only wanted them to show me the scroll. That's why I said that," protested Seikei.

"But when they didn't let you see it, you surely returned here to ask the emperor—"

"And then took him away," the first minister cried out, as if seeing the plot clearly.

"Because he *refused* to give the order," said the second one.

"I think there is another explanation," Yabuta said. He signaled his guards to bring someone else from the pagoda. Seikei was astounded when he saw who it was.

7 — Facing the Short Sword

Walking down the hill, bowing respectfully at everyone he passed, was Takanori, the ronin Seikei had met on the road to Kyoto. He looked a little better than when Seikei had seen him last, apparently having benefited from a bath and a change of clothing.

He bowed before Seikei, the two ministers, and finally—with the deepest bow of all—to Yabuta. Evidently Takanori had a good idea who was in charge here.

"Have you ever seen this young man before?" Yabuta asked Takanori.

Takanori looked briefly at Seikei, and replied, "Oh, certainly, Your Honor. Two days ago, on the Tokaido Road."

"What did you tell him?"

"Something of great importance, sir. I told him the same thing I told you."

"Which was?"

"That my daimyo, Lord Shima, had suffered a great—"

"Not that. What *else* did you tell him?"

"You mean about Lord Ponzu?"

"Yes." Yabuta was impatient, Seikei saw. No doubt he was very quick to use torture if he suspected someone he was questioning was too slow with the truth.

Takanori licked his lips, trying to get this part of the story right. "Well, I reported that Lord Ponzu, whose men had killed my daimyo, was plotting an uprising against the shogun."

"And what did this young samurai *do,*" Yabuta asked, "when you reported this startling piece of information to him?"

"Oh, he bought me some soup." Takanori bowed his head at Seikei to thank him again.

"Did he tell you to come with him to Edo so you could report it to the shogun's officials?" asked Yabuta.

"No, he was very busy, sir. He had to get here to Kyoto in a hurry."

Yabuta turned to Seikei. "And when you arrived here, did you report this startling news to the governor, as was your duty?"

"No," said Seikei. "I didn't find this man's story believable."

"But that wasn't for *you* to decide, was it?" Yabuta asked. His tone was icy. "Are you one of the shogun's magistrates, who are authorized to investigate such matters?"

Seikei shook his head. Yabuta was correct, of course, but he was twisting everything. Seikei recalled the judge's warning outside the shogun's castle in Edo.

"You're wasting time," Seikei said. "The emperor has been kidnapped and—"

"Yes, tell us about that, won't you? Be truthful now and I will go easy on you."

"I couldn't have had anything to do with that!" Seikei protested. "Ask the guard who went with me to the palace. From there, we went back to the governor's residence."

"I have already asked him," Yabuta said. "He did leave you at the governor's, but you could easily have returned *here* by yourself, since you had learned the way."

"You can't believe that! Why would I want to kill these monks? What would I do with the emperor?"

Yabuta leaned closer to Seikei. His voice was lower now, as if he wanted it to be heard by Seikei alone. "I'll tell you what I do believe," he said. "You met this man on the road and he told you of a plot against the shogun. I have heard that you like to solve crimes as if *you,* not your foster father, were the judge. He isn't here to lend you the cover of his authority, so you decided you would do this on your own. You took on something that was too big for you, in order to bring glory upon yourself."

Yabuta's voice had taken on a singsong quality, like the sound of a loom when a weaver is making cloth. It was as if he were weaving a terrible blanket of lies and truth to ensnare Seikei.

"You should have reported the plot," said Yabuta. "You didn't. Then you learned while you were here that the emperor was planning to escape—and instead of bringing that information to the governor, you went looking for the scroll so you could present the proof of the plot yourself."

"I realized that he had plans to control the emperor," added the Minister of the Left, pointing at Seikei.

"What have you done with him?" asked the other minister.

Annoyed, Yabuta motioned for a guard. "Take these two and put them someplace where they can't talk to anyone," he ordered.

As they were led away, the two ministers now resembled squawking chickens more than peacocks. Seikei's satisfaction at the sight, however, was fleeting.

"Because you failed to perform your duty," Yabuta

told him, "a serious threat against the shogun—who trusted you—has arisen."

"What threat?" Seikei demanded. "You can't really believe this man's story." He pointed to the ronin, who bowed.

"You know only a part of what is happening," Yabuta replied.

"And I deny having anything to do with the emperor's disappearance," Seikei said.

Yabuta's dark, cold eyes opened wide. Seikei had to force himself not to shrink from them. He felt he was looking into a lake with no bottom. "But you allowed him to get away," Yabuta said. "And free, he is dangerous."

"I can't imagine anyone *less* dangerous," said Seikei.

"No one cares what *you* imagine," replied Yabuta.

"I will report to the governor—" Seikei began.

Yabuta cut him off. "He knows all about you already. In addition to your failure to inform him about a planned rebellion, you have other offenses. I have innkeepers' bills showing that you ordered lavish meals at every stop between here and Edo. You demanded service fit for a daimyo, not for a courier who was supposed to be carrying out a task for the shogun."

Seikei hung his head. He could not deny the truth of

this, even though Yabuta made it sound worse than it had been.

"Wait," Seikei said. "There was another man here yesterday. He may have heard what I said to the emperor. He could confirm—"

"Where is this man now?" snapped Yabuta.

"I don't know, but he was dressed in a blue kimono, and he left two swords with the guard at the temple porch." Seikei hesitated. "At least I think they were his."

Yabuta curled his lip. "That's hardly a precise description. No one else reported seeing this other samurai. Perhaps you imagined him."

Seikei wanted to protest, but he saw that was useless. He bowed his head. "Then how may I help find the emperor?" he asked humbly.

"Find the emperor?" Yabuta didn't try to suppress the gloating in his voice. "I don't believe I need any more of your *help*." He licked his lips, and asked, "Are you familiar with the saying, 'A samurai has two swords. When the long one fails, the short one must succeed'?"

"Yes," Seikei said after a pause. He knew what Yabuta meant.

"The guards will take you back to your room," said Yabuta. "I suggest you consider what the effect would be if your disgrace is made public. Your foster father, Judge Ooka, will be humiliated as well. You—and only you—could spare him that."

Seikei understood the meaning behind that as well. Numbly, he followed the guards, wondering how he could have made so many mistakes. The judge had even warned him about Yabuta, which made Seikei's failure all the harder to bear.

At the governor's residence, the guards took Seikei's horse and left him at the guesthouse. They let him keep his swords, of course. Yabuta intended him to use them, or at least one of them.

That was the meaning of the saying Yabuta had referred to. If a samurai failed to overcome his enemy with the long sword that he carried, then it was his duty to use the short one—on himself.

Seikei had always believed that he would, if necessary, preserve his honor in this manner. He had never seen a samurai actually commit *seppuku,* although he did witness the actor Tomomi kneel and bare his neck for the sword. Tomomi had been strong-willed and entirely willing to die, for he had accomplished his goal. He did not hesitate to accept death as the price of honor.

But Seikei had heard stories of other samurai who,

when called on to end their own lives, could not bring themselves to do it. Some asked a faithful retainer to cut off their heads. Others tried to stab themselves, but did such a poor job that they lay in agony, waiting to bleed to death.

Seikei withdrew his short sword from its scabbard and looked at it. It was a fine sword, given to him as a present by the governor of Yamato Province because Seikei had defeated the ninja named Kitsune. The governor had, in turn, won the pair of swords long ago from Seikei's father Judge Ooka.

Tears came to Seikei's eyes as he thought of the man he respected more than any other. What would the judge feel when he learned that Seikei had disgraced himself? Would he approve of Seikei's decision to commit seppuku? Would seppuku prove that Seikei's only desire was to honor his foster father?

A memory floated into Seikei's mind like a blackbird flying across a gray sky before a storm. He had often discussed with the judge the duties of a samurai. On one occasion, Seikei had been reading one of the many books devoted to the subject. "Those books have fine thoughts in them," the judge had said. "But a man knows best of all, in his heart, what his duty is and whether he has fulfilled it or not."

Seikei turned the sword over in his hand, looking at its gleaming edge, which was sharp enough to cut a falling leaf in two. He thought about what the judge had said.

There was still another way.

8 —
Driving a Hard Bargain

Seikei used his short sword to cut his hair so that he would no longer be recognized as a samurai. Then he made a *hachimaki* headband, inscribed it with the word *honor,* and tied it around his forehead. By doing so, he signaled that he had pledged to wear it until he had accomplished his task.

No one noticed him as he slipped out of the guesthouse and left the grounds of the governor's residence. Yabuta had not thought it worthwhile to put a guard on him. If Seikei chose to flee rather than kill himself, that was only one more indication of his unworthiness to serve the shogun.

Seikei knew where he must go first. In the city where he spent his boyhood, there were shops where people in need could obtain loans if they left something valuable behind. It was possible to pay back the loan, plus a fee, within a certain period of time and regain whatever had been left.

There must be such places in Kyoto, Seikei knew, and he found one not far from the governor's residence. The owner, an elderly man whose face looked like a piece of ancient porcelain with a network of fine cracks in it, didn't even seem surprised when Seikei offered his swords.

"Going into business?" asked the old man as he examined the blades.

Seikei did not answer. His stomach was churning at the thought of leaving the swords here. When Seikei put aside his old wooden sword and took up these, made by a craftsman from the finest steel, he had truly become a samurai. If he failed to accomplish what he had in mind, then he would never be able to redeem the swords. That would not only bring greater shame on Seikei's head, but make it impossible for him to die honorably by committing seppuku.

The old man counted out twenty *ryo* onto the counter and looked up. Seikei realized that was far less than the swords were worth. But what could he do about it? He recalled that his father the tea merchant had always complained that Seikei had a poor head for business.

"Anyone can cheat you!" Father had wailed. "You will lose everything I've saved in my entire life."

So Seikei forced himself to shake his head no. The old man acted insulted. Seikei had seen his father do that when a customer refused to pay the asking price for tea.

Seikei reached for the swords as if to take them away.

The old man put another ten ryo on the counter. Seikei waited, still not saying anything.

The old man sighed. "I'll tell you what," he said. "If you leave your kosode too, I can give you another five ryo. As long as you're giving up your swords, you won't need that jacket. You won't be in the shogun's service anymore."

Seikei realized he was right. "I'll need something else to wear," he muttered. He looked around the shop. "How about that?" he said, pointing to a *happu,* a plain blue jacket of the kind shopkeepers' delivery boys used.

"You looking for a job?" the old man asked.

"I have one already," Seikei replied.

He left the shop feeling slightly dizzy. He kept reaching to his waist, feeling the loss of weight caused by his missing swords. But there was no time for regrets. He knew that before he could accomplish anything else, he had to find out what the Kusanagi scroll contained.

In a street near the imperial palace, Seikei bought a small basket of pears from a farmer who had brought a cartload into the city. Seikei knew that even though the emperor was missing, there were many other people who lived and worked at the palace—members of the imperial family, officials, clerks, servants. They all had to be fed, and someone carrying food into the grounds would not arouse suspicion.

By the smell, he found the entrance that led to the kitchen. As he expected, it was large and chaotically busy, with rows of chefs cleaning fish, steam rising from pots of rice in fireplaces, and servants carrying trays out as soon as they were filled. No one gave Seikei a second glance as he put down his pears and picked up one of the trays.

He assumed that the library would be in that part of the palace close to the hall of the two chief ministers. Neither of them would wish to walk far to obtain a scroll. Luckily, he found his way to the corridor he remembered from the day before. He only hoped that Yabuta had kept the two ministers in custody so that Seikei wouldn't encounter them.

A female servant emerged from a doorway and walked toward Seikei. She was young and frowned when she saw him, as if realizing he was out of place. He tried to make himself appear as stupid as possible. "Library? Library?" he asked in a high voice.

She turned and pointed to a door at the other end of the hallway. Seikei bowed—nearly spilling the tray—and thanked her profusely. When he reached the doorway, he looked over his shoulder and saw that she had waited to see that he entered the right room.

He slid the door open and stepped inside. Around the walls were shelves holding hundreds of scrolls of all sizes. Some looked too large for one person to lift; others were small enough to fit in the sleeve of a kimono. Each one had a title on the end. In the center of the room were some mats where one could sit, and at the far end, large windows let sunlight in.

Fortunately, no one else was here. Seikei set the tray down and started to read the titles of the scrolls, looking for the one that read *Kusanagi*. It seemed like a hopeless task. At any moment someone might come in. The girl who had seen him might have reported it to someone else. . . .

Then Seikei's eye fell on a lacquered table that held

several scrolls that had not been reshelved. Of course! Yabuta had read the Kusanagi scroll, because the two ministers had shown it to him. Seikei examined the loose scrolls and felt a thrill when he lifted the one titled *Kusanagi.*

What to do now? Even though it was one of the smaller scrolls, he had no time to read it here. Taking it was risky too, for someone might search him. He decided that it couldn't be helped. He must find out what message the scroll contained. Concealing it under his jacket, Seikei slid open the door and peered into the corridor. It was empty. He slipped out and headed for the kitchen.

On the way, he heard people shouting. He stopped, fearing that someone had already discovered the missing scroll. But then he realized the noise came from outside the palace. It had nothing to do with him.

By the time Seikei reached the kitchen, two palace guards were there, questioning the cooks. He tensed, preparing to run if they remembered he had been at the palace yesterday.

But as he listened, he realized the guards were looking for someone who had broken into a shrine on the palace grounds. Evidently it was a shrine that was used very rarely, and only today had someone discovered that the door to it had been forced open.

No one in the kitchen reported noticing anything strange. Seikei, in his happu jacket, slipped out the door as if going about his ordinary business. As he approached the castle gate through which he had entered the grounds, however, he slowed his pace. A line of people had formed because guards were searching everyone who passed through.

"They're trying to find something that was stolen from the shrine," Seikei heard someone behind him say. He looked back to see two tradesmen with empty handcarts. They had delivered their wares to the palace and were now eager to return home.

"Yes," the second one said. "Look, there are two Shinto priests with the guards. You don't often see them away from the shrines."

"I heard the shrine that was broken into was the Sacred Purple Hall," said the first one.

"Very holy place," commented the other. "They use it only when a new emperor is enthroned, you know."

The first man lowered his voice. Seikei took a step backward to listen. "I heard a rumor about the emperor," the man said. He went on, but whispering now so that Seikei could no longer make out his words. Probably he was repeating what Seikei already knew—that the emperor was missing and the nation, for now at least, had no link with the goddess Amaterasu.

Meanwhile, the scroll under Seikei's jacket felt as uncomfortable as a burning stick. Even though it wasn't the sacred object the guards were looking for, they would certainly discover it when they searched him. Someone would recognize it as belonging to the palace library, and Seikei had no way to explain what he was doing with it.

He dropped back farther in the line. Now the two gossiping tradesmen were ahead of him. Clearly they had nothing to fear. The guards' inspection was merely an annoying delay to them. Each of the men pulled a wooden two-wheeled cart with only a shallow layer of straw in the bottom.

Desperate, Seikei had a sudden inspiration. He reached over the side of one of the carts and worked the scroll out from his sleeve, dropping it out the end. He rapidly brushed some of the straw over it. Feeling the slight movement of Seikei's hand, the man pulling the cart half turned and gave Seikei a curious look. Seikei removed a single straw and used it to clean his ear. Satisfied that nothing was amiss, the man returned to the conversation with his friend.

Seikei followed a few steps behind, preparing to look innocent when he was inspected by the guards—and conscious that he wasn't doing a very good job of it. He was sweating; he felt weak-kneed and almost stumbled because he was dizzy with apprehension. Instinctively he reached for the reassuring touch of his swords to remind himself to act like a samurai, but of course they were gone.

The tradesmen, as he had hoped, experienced no trouble passing through the gate. They slipped off their kimonos and shook them out, exchanging good-natured banter with the samurai inspecting them. After a glance inside the carts, the guards waved the men through.

Seikei tried to appear just as calm, removing his jacket and the monohiki he wore around his legs. The guards took their time, inspecting the quilted jacket for any hidden pockets. Seikei, shivering as the cold air puckered his skin, suppressed a desire to tell the guards to hurry, as he would have only yesterday when he was dressed in the shogun's hollyhock cloth. He hoped that the tradesmen would still be in sight by the time he passed this inspection.

At last the guards decided Seikei had nothing to hide. He pulled on the monohiki as quickly as possible, and then ran through the gate, slipping into his jacket. With relief he saw the two tradesmen and their carts at the far end of the street. As he hurried toward them, Seikei's heart jumped. The man whose cart held the scroll had chosen this moment to stop and smooth out the straw in the back. As Seikei watched in dismay, the man picked up the scroll and showed it to his friend.

9 — Settling an Argument

By the time Seikei caught up to the tradesmen, they were arguing. "We should take this straight back to the guards," the one holding the scroll said. "Otherwise we'll get into trouble."

The second one shook his head. "That's exactly the way you *will* get into trouble," he said. "First off, they'll ask how you came into possession of what is clearly not your property."

"Well, I can answer that I happened to find it in my cart."

The second one snorted. "Think they'll believe that? No, very likely you stole it and when you found you couldn't sell it, you brought it back to collect a reward."

The first man looked worried. "Well, what do *you* think I should do with it?"

"Best to leave it at a shrine and let the kami dispose of it as they please."

As Seikei knelt a short distance away, pretending to adjust his sandals, he saw the first man unroll the scroll a little. "Look at that," he said to the other. "Beautiful calligraphy. Probably it's *worth* a reward."

The second man took a brief glance and then turned his head away. "Too fancy for me," he commented. "You couldn't even read it."

"Well, reading it's not the *point* of calligraphy," responded his friend. "It's the beauty that matters."

Seikei couldn't endure listening to this any longer. He went over to the carts. "What's that you've got there?" he asked the man with the scroll.

The man halfheartedly attempted to hide it behind his back. "Why do you want to know?" he asked, peering suspiciously at Seikei. Seikei hoped the man wouldn't remember who had been walking behind him at the castle.

But he did. "Say," he said with a crafty look, "didn't I see you earlier?"

"Just before you slipped through the gate with that scroll hidden in your wagon?" said Seikei. "You fellows were pretty clever to get away with it, I'd say."

The second man took a step backward. "Don't include *me* in this," he said. "I never saw this man until today."

The man with the scroll looked hurt. "Yoshi," he said to the other man, "haven't we sold our goods together at the palace every week for seven years . . . maybe eight?"

"Oh, was that you? I never noticed."

"You know," Seikei said, "I have a feeling that scroll is just what the guards at the palace were looking for."

It now appeared as if the man with the scroll felt as if he'd put his hand into his cart and pulled out a snake.

"In fact," Seikei went on, "I would think they'd pay a reward for it."

The pain on the man's face suddenly turned into a smile. "That's just what I was saying . . . to this strange fellow Yoshi who never saw me before today."

"I still think you're inviting trouble," muttered Yoshi.

"I tell you what," said Seikei, trying his best to look honest and stupid at the same time. "Why don't you let me take the scroll back to the guards and see if they will pay a reward for it? That way, if there's any suspicion, it won't fall on you."

"How will you account for having the scroll?" Yoshi asked.

"I'll just say I found it in the street," responded Seikei. "They have to believe that, because they searched me to the skin when I left."

"How about that?" the man with the scroll asked his friend Yoshi.

"What do we get out of this?" Yoshi asked Seikei.

"We?" said the first man. "I thought you never—"

"You can wait here," Seikei said quickly. "Where it's *safe,*" he stressed. "Then I'll come back with the reward and we'll split it three ways."

"I don't know if you should get a full equal share," said Yoshi. "After all, 'twas us who found the scroll."

"Us?" said the man holding the scroll.

"Well," said Seikei smoothly, reaching his hand out in as reassuring a way as he could, "you can just give me whatever you think is fair."

"Right," the first man said, and he plopped the scroll into Seikei's outstretched hand. In truth, he seemed glad to be rid of it.

The second man still wanted to negotiate the precise division of the reward, but now that Seikei actually had the scroll, he didn't hesitate. "Whatever you think is fair," Seikei repeated, and he headed off toward the palace gate.

There was a growing crowd in that part of the street, for the people trying to get inside were slowed by the line waiting to get out. Seikei had no trouble disappearing from sight, and then slipping out the other side of the throng. The street then curved around to the other side of the palace. It was not so heavily traveled here because it was narrower and more difficult for carts to pass through. Probably the two tradesmen had never taken that route and had forgotten it was here.

Seikei felt relieved when he reached the next intersection and turned right. There were no shouts behind him. He was a little ashamed of himself, and wondered how long the two men would wait for him to return. He told himself that at least they would lose nothing—except maybe their friendship. Seikei had only stolen from them what was rightfully . . . well, what he had *earlier* stolen from the palace. So who had a better right to it?

Now he had to find someplace to stop and try to read the scroll. Sooner or later someone would discover it was missing. Seikei remembered that the library had seemed deserted, but what if it were really true that Yabuta could place an eye there? He would have seen Seikei take it, and even now might have sent guards to pursue him.

Seikei glanced over his shoulder. All he saw was a geisha out for a walk, dressed in a fine kimono and twirling a paper umbrella to protect her skin from the sun. He looked more closely, thinking it might actually be Bunzo, the judge's faithful samurai. Once, Bunzo had worn a disguise to follow Seikei along the Tokaido Road to ensure he would not get into trouble.

Seikei banished the thought from his mind. He was in plenty of trouble now and it was unworthy to expect Bunzo to get him out of it. Seikei had to do the job himself.

He turned another corner and came to a quiet street with a few small pottery shops and a Shinto shrine. This would be as good a spot as any to examine the scroll.

Walking through the *torii* gate that marked the entrance to the shrine, Seikei clapped his hands. This was intended to draw the attention of the kami who resided there. Sometimes the noise attracted a Shinto priest, who would appear to receive a donation.

This time, none did. Seikei had the feeling that he was alone here, except of course for the spirit who occupied the *honden*. This was a small wooden building that usually surrounded some natural object—a rock, a tree, or a place that had been identified as one of the sacred spots where Heaven and Earth met.

No one other than the priests was allowed inside the

honden. When ordinary people assembled here for religious festivals, they gathered in the gravel courtyard outside. Here it was that Seikei sat, folded his legs, and carefully began to unroll the scroll. Despite the emperor's taunting, Seikei was eager to find the secret it contained.

10 — The Invincible Kusanagi

The language of the scroll was more difficult than Seikei had expected. He remembered one of the two ministers telling him that he could not read it. The problem wasn't just the elaborate calligraphy. Seikei was an admirer of the artistic styles of writing, and he could usually determine what any of them meant.

But this was apparently a very old form of language. Seikei had heard that members of the priesthood and certain palace officials had to be trained to read ancient literature.

He had no time for that. He concentrated on the symbols, trying to make sense of them. He said a prayer to the kami that inhabited the shrine. After a time, the pattern became clearer. It was as if a mist in the forest suddenly lifted and Seikei found himself in a beautiful world that was somehow different from any other place he had ever seen. . . .

It was in the time before time began, before Ninigi came to rule the land of Nippon. Amaterasu reigned over Heaven and Earth and all the other kami paid homage to her. All except her brother, the mischievous Susanoo, who was jealous of his sister's power and beauty. Susanoo stomped through Heaven, causing thunder and lightning to appear in the sky. He opened the floodgates, sending torrents of rain to Earth, ruining the rice paddies. He made volcanoes erupt and tore the land asunder with earthquakes. Finally, he came to Amaterasu's weaving hall and threw a horse inside, causing everyone to scatter in terror.

Frightened and upset, Amaterasu withdrew into a cave. The sun disappeared, and darkness engulfed Heaven and Earth. The other kami gathered and begged her to come out, but they had no success. Even Susanoo regretted what he had done.

The kami decided on a trick. Someone hung a mirror on a tree outside the cave. The goddess Uzume performed a dance that made all the other kami laugh. Curious, Amaterasu came to the entrance of the cave and peeped out. Seeing her own reflection in the mirror, she emerged to see who such a beautiful spirit was. Two of the strongest kami clasped her hands and would not let her return to the cave. That was the origin of the sacred mirror.

To celebrate Amaterasu's return, the other kami presented her with a beautiful jewel. That was the origin of the sacred jewel.

The kami decided that Susanoo must be punished for his ac-

tions, and banished him to Earth. They told him he must stay there until he atoned for the trouble he caused. He wandered through the world until he encountered an old couple and their daughter. Weeping, the couple explained that a dragon with eight tails had stolen seven of their daughters and would soon return for this one.

Susanoo tricked the dragon into drinking a barrel of wine so that it fell asleep. He then used his sword to cut off each of the dragon's tails. Inside the last one he discovered another sword, one of great power. He returned to Heaven and presented it to his sister so that she would forgive him. That was the origin of the sacred sword.

At a later time, Amaterasu sent Ninigi, one of her sons, to descend to Earth and rule the land. As a sign of her authority, she gave him three gifts: the mirror that drew her from the cave, the jewel that the other kami gave her, and the sword found by Susanoo.

Ninigi's son Jimmu became the first emperor and received the three gifts, passing them on to his son when he died. And so it was done until the time of the twelfth emperor, named Keiko. When Keiko realized that not all the people had accepted his authority, he called for his son Yamato. He gave the sacred sword to Yamato and told him to conquer all the lands he could find.

Yamato set out to obey his father's command. Soon many more lands had been brought into the emperor's domain. But the enemies of Yamato plotted to kill him. They waited until he was riding through a vast plain of dry grass. Then they surrounded him and set the grass on fire. Seeing the danger, Yamato drew his sword and cut down the burning grass. Afterward, he cut off the heads of as many enemies as there had been blades of grass. And so the sword became known as Kusanagi—"the sword that cut the burning grass."

After Yamato completed his conquest of all the lands, he placed the sword in the Atsuta Shrine at Nagoya. Yamato feared that anyone who came into possession of the sword would gain its power. So he placed a spell on it to make sure that only a descendant of Amaterasu would have the ability to remove it from its resting place.

The other two gifts of Amaterasu, the mirror and the jewel, are kept in the imperial palace. They are used, along with a replica of the sword, in the ceremony for enthroning a new emperor.

At the end of the manuscript, in a form of calligraphy that was obviously done by a different person, was written:

No one but the high priest shall learn of this.

Seikei shivered and looked around him, surprised to have returned to the world he usually lived in. The sun had disappeared, but only because a storm was blowing up late in the afternoon. Cascades of autumn leaves were losing their last grip on the trees. As they fell, they surrounded Seikei on the gravel courtyard. Seikei thought of Amaterasu and her brother Susanoo, about the thousands of warriors who fell like blades of grass when Yamato wielded the mighty sword named Kusanagi.

Some parts of this story he had heard before. Seikei's mother had told him about the creation of the world and that the emperor was descended from Amaterasu. Seikei himself had visited the shrine of Ise and asked for Amaterasu's aid when he pursued the actor Tomomi along the Tokaido Road.

But he had never heard the story of the sword that cut the burning grass. Nor did he understand how it explained why the emperor—Risu, the Squirrel—believed he wasn't really the emperor.

Of course, Risu had told Seikei that he wouldn't understand. So had the Ministers of the Right and Left, or at least one of them had. The other one had said, "And even if you *did* understand . . ."

What? Had the minister finished the sentence? Seikei couldn't be certain.

If he did understand, maybe he couldn't *do* anything

about it? Yabuta seemed to have understood the message in the scroll. He was doing something about it. But what?

Seikei decided not to worry about that right now. What he *had* to do was find the emperor and bring him back before Yabuta could. Unfortunately, the scroll gave no clues as to where the emperor was now.

Or did it? The shrine mentioned in it . . . Atsuta Shrine at Nagoya. If the emperor wanted to gain the power of the sword, might he have gone there?

Somehow, Seikei thought, the Squirrel didn't seem like a person who wanted to gain power. Possession of a bowl of ginkgo porridge was enough power for him.

But of course, *someone* had killed the two monks. That certainly had not been the Squirrel, no matter what Yabuta believed. So if whoever did it knew about this scroll, maybe they were on the way to Nagoya, taking the emperor along. The Squirrel might have learned that not everyone was reluctant to force him to do things.

A flash of lightning streaked through the sky, followed a moment later by a clap of thunder. Susanoo would romp through Heaven tonight, thought Seikei.

11 — Amaterasu Appears

The storm came on swiftly, accompanied by a cold wind, a reminder that winter would soon be here. Shopkeepers rushed to lower the bamboo curtains in front of their stores to keep the rain from coming in. Seikei searched the nearby streets in vain for an inn. Either he was in the wrong part of the city, or the inns had filled up early and taken down their signs.

By now Seikei's clothes were sopping wet. The wind chilled him through, and he began to shiver. In desperation he went up an alleyway and crawled into an empty barrel that was lying on its side. Here at least he was sheltered from the storm, and could sleep.

All night long, however, crashes of thunder and the howling wind awakened him. He dreamed that Susanoo, with the fierce face of a demon, was beating on the sides of the barrel. Seikei scrunched up, trying to collect as much warmth as possible.

When he awoke, his clothes were still damp, but now he felt warm. Uncomfortably so, and he ached all over. The only good thing was that the rain had stopped and the sun shone through the open end of the barrel.

Then a shadow fell across the sun, startling Seikei enough to make him look. A face was there, staring back at him from the center of the sun. A woman's face. Amaterasu? He tried to speak her name, but only a croak escaped from his throat.

"What are you doing in there?" she asked.

Seikei attempted to smile, but wasn't sure he succeeded. Amaterasu must be joking with him, for she knew everything that went on. Everything there was to know. . . .

The next time he awoke, he was inside, in a room. It was hot, but someone had put a quilt over him. He wanted to cool off. He was sweating. He tried to throw the quilt off, but it was too heavy.

Then Amaterasu appeared again. "Drink this," she said, helping him sit up. The liquid in the cup she held to his lips was hot too, and at first he didn't want it. But after he tasted a little, he realized it was good. It would help him grow strong. His mother had made him some tea like this when he was very little, so that he would get well and become strong. Strong enough to throw off the quilt.

He slept some more. Now it was dark again, but Susanoo had gone away and the heavens were peaceful. Seikei realized he no longer felt hot, but he was still weak. He remembered that Amaterasu had visited him and he wondered if that had been only a dream. It seemed important. He tried to think why. It had something to do with the scroll.

The scroll! He sat up suddenly and realized that someone had taken his clothes and, along with them, the scroll.

He started to think. Obviously whoever had found him had not simply desired to rob him. Otherwise he would not be lying under a quilt in a warm room. But where was he? He clapped his hands, thinking that would attract Amaterasu again.

The sound faded away in the darkness, and nothing happened. Seikei thought about getting up, but it was comfortable here, and as long as no one was going to appear . . .

The door to the room slid open and Amaterasu was there, holding a candle. This time, though, Seikei could see that she was only a girl, a year or two younger than he was—too young yet to have her hair drawn up and pinned in a woman's style. Instead, it hung down on either side of her face, making it seem as round as the moon.

"I thought I heard something," she said. "Are you feeling better?"

"Yes," Seikei said. "But I'm hungry." All at once he realized that he had a terribly empty feeling in his stomach.

"I can't get you anything until morning except some pickled *daikon* root," the girl said.

"Whatever you have will be fine," replied Seikei.

The girl nodded and disappeared. When she returned, bringing the sliced daikon root, Seikei found its tartness delicious. "I am sorry we have so little to give you," the girl said. "The kitchen fire has been banked for the night."

Seikei found her apology strange. "Where am I?" he asked.

"This is the house of Moriyama Yasuo," she replied. "A rice merchant."

"Why did he treat me so generously?"

"Oh, he doesn't know anything about you," she said. "He is away on a business trip."

Seikei blinked. "Well, then . . ."

"I found you in the barrel," the girl explained. "And of course I knew at once who you were."

"You did?"

"Well, of course I knew, because you had that scroll."

"The scroll, yes. Where is it?"

"It's in the cabinet by the wall here. Along with your clothes. I cleaned them myself. Well, Araori helped. She's the other servant. I'm sleeping in her room. This one was mine."

There was something about the conversation that puzzled Seikei. He was still thinking slowly, even after the fever had gone down. "You say you know who I am? Because of the scroll?"

"Well, that wasn't the *only* reason. Everyone has heard you were missing. And the scroll has a chrysanthemum seal on it." She bowed her head. "I could guess where *that* came from."

Seikei nodded slowly. The chrysanthemum was the symbol of the emperor, and this girl must have known he took the scroll from the imperial library. "You haven't told anyone, have you?" Seikei asked anxiously. If the girl knew he was missing, Yabuta must be hunting for him.

"Just Araori. I couldn't hide you from her. But the rest of the household—it's only the merchant's wife and mother—they don't know. As long as we keep the house clean and serve them their meals on time, they take no interest in us. But when the master comes home . . ." She lowered her head.

"When will that be?" asked Seikei.

"Not for several days," replied the girl. "We can be gone by then."

We?

"Oh," she continued, ignoring Seikei's startled look. "That reminds me. Here is your headband." She took it from the sleeve of her kimono. "I protected it, for I knew you would want it."

She tied it around Seikei's forehead. "This was another way I knew who you were," she said, sitting back and giving him an admiring look.

"I see," said Seikei, wondering how he could subtly ask who she thought he was. "What's *your* name?" he said.

"Hato," she answered. "Pigeon. As you know, the pigeon is always a faithful servant of the hero in many stories. She flies ahead and warns him of danger."

"Yes," Seikei said. "Well, of course I wouldn't want to put *you* in danger. And besides, your master needs you here."

"He beats me," she said.

"He does? I can hardly believe—" Seikei stopped because Hato had turned away from him and lowered her kimono. Ugly bruises and welts marked the skin on her back.

"He shouldn't be allowed to do that," Seikei said.

Hato rearranged her clothing and faced him. "He can do anything he wishes," she said. "For I have no other place to go."

Seikei knew this must be true. "But you can't come with *me.* It would be too . . . difficult."

Hato knelt before Seikei, despite his protests. "I swear to you," she said, "that I will not be a burden. I will kill myself rather than reveal your secret."

Seikei took a deep breath. He remembered what the judge had said about not wanting to have too much responsibility.

"What do you think my secret is?" he asked.

Hato started to respond, then caught herself. She smiled. "I see," she said. "You were testing me. No, I will never let your secret pass my lips."

12 — Danger on the Road

Hato served as the cook for the household. Her master would miss her, Seikei thought as he sipped the last of the fish and seaweed broth she had made. It tasted so good that even the judge would have enjoyed it.

It was the early morning of the following day. The sun had not yet risen, but the two of them planned to slip out of the house before anyone else had awakened. Hato's friend Araori knew of their intentions, but fortunately (from Seikei's point of view), she would rather remain a servant than go on a journey with "chrysanthemum boy," as she called Seikei.

Most of Seikei's strength had returned, but when he stepped outside, he felt a pang of doubt. Fog had settled close to the ground between the houses, making it seem as if he and Hato were in an empty wilderness. He wondered if they were setting out on some mad quest. Would the judge approve of this? Perhaps Seikei should have used the short sword after all.

He shook his head to clear it. "Follow the path," the judge always said. The path led to the Atsuta Shrine. Seikei must do his utmost to reach it. He and Hato passed through the city gate without being questioned, and once again Seikei found himself on the great Tokaido Road.

At this hour the road was lightly traveled. The fog stubbornly remained, making the scene around them look like gray cotton, only occasionally marked by splashes of color when a tree branch pierced the mist.

Seeming nervous for the first time, Hato told Seikei about her life. She remembered nothing of her parents. They had been lost in a flood, and Hato's grandmother raised her until she was six. Then, because the grandmother needed money to feed Hato's two brothers, she sold Hato to the rice merchant. At that time, he had an elderly woman as his cook. He wanted her to teach Hato everything she knew.

Unfortunately, the cook died before Hato's training was finished. Her master completed the cooking course by beating her whenever she prepared a dish he did not like.

"But you're a fine cook now," said Seikei. "Why is he still beating you?"

"He grew to like it, I think," she replied. "His business hasn't gone well, and he drinks too much sake. When that happens, his wife hides herself and he comes searching for me."

"I can see why you wanted to leave him," Seikei said. "With your skills, you should be able to find a job cooking for another merchant, or even a samurai."

She glanced at him with a shy smile. "Why should I work for them when I can follow you?"

"Well, for one thing, I can't pay you very much," he said. "And after I'm finished with my task, well . . ." He didn't want to face the fact that he might never finish what he had set out to do.

"After you've finished," Hato said, "I will accompany you to the palace. You must need many servants there."

The palace? Seikei suddenly realized who she thought he was. But before he could correct her, he heard heavy footsteps behind them in the fog. Turning to see what it was, he realized that someone was coming from the other direction too.

The figures of three men emerged from the fog, surrounding Seikei and Hato. Two of them carried clubs;

the third, a heavy staff. Seikei knew at once that they were bandits who preyed on helpless travelers.

"Give us your valuables," one of them said, "and we won't hurt you."

Seikei's first thought was to save Hato from harm. He reached for the bag in which he carried the money he had received for the swords.

Hato put her hand on his arm. "Tell them who you are," she said.

"Ah . . . no, I'll just give them my money. It isn't much," Seikei said. He held out the bag and one of the men snatched it.

"What else do you have?" the man who seemed to be the leader asked.

"Nothing," said Seikei. "We're only—"

"There's a pittance in here," said the man who had taken the bag. "They must have more." Seikei glanced at Hato. She had wanted to carry the scroll, and foolishly he had allowed her.

"The girl must be hiding it," the leader said. "Search her."

As the third man reached for Hato, she screamed and twisted out of his grasp.

Automatically, Seikei reached for his sword, cursing

his stupidity when his hand clasped only air. "Stop it!" he shouted. "I command you . . . in the name of the emperor." No one paid any attention.

One of the bandits had caught Hato. "Call the kami," she shouted at Seikei as she struggled to free herself.

Almost without thinking, Seikei clapped his hands together.

Another figure appeared then, a tall gray-haired man wearing a plain blue kimono and two swords. Seikei was astonished. Never in his lifetime had a kami actually *appeared* when he clapped his hands.

Then Seikei recognized him.

"What's going on here?" the man said.

"Help us!" Hato screamed as the bandit holding her tried to cover her mouth.

"Let her go." The man in the blue kimono spoke with the kind of authority Seikei wished *he* had. Looking at him more closely, Seikei was sure of it: This was the man he had seen at the Kinkakuji monastery the day he had met the emperor.

The bandit released Hato. He and the other two drew closer together. It was clear they were wondering how strong an opponent the man in blue would be.

Hato shouted at him, "They took our money. Make them return it."

The stranger withdrew his long sword part of the way from its scabbard, showing its sharp edge. The bandits knew that if he exposed it completely he would be compelled to shed blood with it. *Their* blood.

The bandit who had taken Seikei's money tossed the bag on the ground. "Too little to bother about," he said.

"Is that all they stole?" the stranger asked.

"Yes," said Hato. "Aren't you going to strike them dead?"

"Not if they run away," the man replied.

The bandits turned and disappeared even more quickly than they had arrived.

"Thank you," said Seikei. He realized that he had stopped breathing.

The man looked him over. "It is dangerous to be out here this early with no weapons or protector," he said.

"That's why he called you," said Hato.

Seikei cringed. He hoped the man wouldn't ask what she meant. "We are on our way to Nagoya," Seikei said, trying to change the subject.

"I am also," the man replied. "You can travel with me if you wish."

Hato nodded as if she had expected nothing less. "My name is Hato," she said. "I am a loyal servant of the emperor."

The man looked at her with a slight smile. "As are we all," he said. "You may call me Reigen."

"I'm Seikei," Seikei muttered.

Hato put her hand over her mouth to conceal a smile and then said, "I'm sure Reigen knows who you really are."

13 —
The Message of the Scroll

Fortunately, Reigen did not inquire into Seikei's "real" identity. On this part of the road, there were many excellent views of Lake Biwa. The sails of its fishing fleets, the picturesque bridges, and the countless wild birds were all favorite subjects for artists. Reigen knew quite a lot about these views, and pointed them out as the three of them walked along.

Unfortunately, Seikei was too distracted to pay close attention. He wanted to tell Hato that he, Seikei, was definitely *not* the emperor. But it would be awkward to do that with Reigen there, for he would think both of them fools.

He also wanted to ask Reigen if he had overheard Seikei and the real emperor talking at the monastery. If so, Reigen could clear Seikei's name—at least, if Yabuta would believe him. On the other hand, Seikei worried that Reigen himself might have had something to do with the murders at the monastery. From the way he had driven off the bandits on the road, it was clear he was an experienced swordsman.

Seikei remained on the alert every time someone approached them from behind. He still feared that when Yabuta learned the scroll was missing from the palace, he might have sent some of the Guards of the Inner Garden to find Seikei.

Once, they had to move to the side of the road and kneel while a large group of samurai rode by on horseback. The crest on their clothing and banners was unfamiliar to Seikei: two shrimp entwined.

He turned his head to see if Reigen recognized the crest, and was horrified to see that the old man wasn't kneeling. Quite the contrary. He was standing with his arms folded, like a commander surveying his forces.

Of course Reigen wore the two swords that marked him as a samurai. But still, it was wise to show proper respect whenever these large bands of warriors passed. Fortunately, their daimyo was not with them, or some of the samurai would have been compelled to challenge Reigen for his boldness. Seikei even saw a couple of them glare meaningfully in Reigen's direction, but they were apparently in too great a hurry to stop.

"You were putting yourself in jeopardy," Seikei said to Reigen after the samurai had passed by.

"Was I?" the old man responded without emotion.

"You failed to show your respect. Any of those samurai could have taken offense."

"I show respect for those who are worthy of it," Reigen replied.

"Did you recognize the crest they wore?"

Reigen nodded. "They were men who serve Lord Ponzu."

Lord Ponzu? Seikei was startled. He recalled the name. That was the daimyo that the ronin Takanori had accused of planning an uprising against the shogun. Of course it was only a coincidence. Lord Ponzu's domain was probably in this vicinity. Still . . . it was unsettling.

"You don't think that Lord Ponzu is worthy of your respect?" Seikei asked Reigen.

"Those were only Lord Ponzu's men. And he himself is only a daimyo," Reigen replied. "What is he compared to the emperor?"

Hato had overheard their conversation. She scolded Reigen, "Yes, but the emperor is in *disguise.* You must be careful not to reveal his secret."

Reigen gave her an odd look. "You may trust me," he said.

The days were growing shorter at this time of year, and it was getting dark. Reigen pointed out a Buddhist monastery where they could spend the night.

"Thanks to you, I still have my money," Seikei said. "I could pay for us to stay at an inn."

"No need for that," Reigen said. "And we will be less conspicuous in a monastery."

Seikei was not eager to attract attention, but wondered briefly why Reigen wished to escape notice as well.

Nevertheless, it was true. Many pilgrims on the way to Nagoya found lodging for the night here. Some were so elderly that they could only walk with the help of relatives. Others were mothers with squalling babies, perhaps taking their children to the Atsuta Shrine to ask the kami to heal them from an illness. There was such a variety of people that no one noticed the three of them. After they ate, Hato went to the women's quarters, and Seikei finally had a chance to speak privately with Reigen.

"I think I have seen you before," Seikei began.

Reigen raised his eyebrows.

"Two days ago, you were at the Kinkakuji monastery in Kyoto. I saw you meditating by the side of the lake."

"You are right," said Reigen.

"I was there talking to a boy who is . . . actually the emperor," Seikei added.

"Ah," Reigen said, nodding. "I remember. Excuse me for failing to recognize you. My eyesight is no longer sharp."

"That night," Seikei went on, "someone killed two of the monks and took the emperor away."

Reigen said nothing. Seikei thought this was extremely strange. Perhaps he had told the old man too much.

"Why did you come to see the emperor?" Reigen finally asked.

Seikei hesitated, but decided that he had to trust Reigen. He was the only person who could help. "I came as a messenger from the shogun. The emperor had refused to perform his duties, and the shogun wanted me to persuade him to return to the palace."

This *did* seem to surprise Reigen. "Why did the shogun choose *you*?" he asked.

Seikei was a little annoyed, but after all, it was the same question he had earlier asked himself. Besides, since he had cut his hair and pawned his swords, he must hardly appear like a samurai's son. "He thought that because the emperor and I are the same age, I might better understand what was bothering him."

"I see," said Reigen, smiling a little. "He thought it must be a problem related to the difficulty of growing up."

"I suppose," said Seikei. He felt Reigen was ever so slightly making fun of him. "But when the emperor disappeared, I was blamed."

"How could that be?"

"The shogun has an official . . ." Again Seikei paused to think. The judge had said it was a crime to mention the name of the Guards of the Inner Garden. But then, Seikei was already in so much trouble that this couldn't make things any worse.

"His name is Yabuta," Seikei revealed. "He is the head of the Guards of the Inner Garden."

Reigen snorted with disgust.

Seikei stared.

"The man that people say has eyes in every room?" Reigen asked.

"How did you know that?"

Reigen shrugged. "He may have eyes even within the imperial palace." That seemed to anger him. "But remember that only Amaterasu truly understands what happens there."

"Well, the thing is," Seikei said, "you could prove I am innocent."

"How could I do that?"

"By returning to Kyoto and telling the governor I had nothing to do with the emperor's disappearance."

Reigen nodded. "But actually," he said, "you did."

Seikei was dumbstruck. He felt as if Reigen had slapped him. "No," he managed to blurt out. "You can't think that."

"I don't mean that you *took* him," explained Reigen. "But someone knew from your arrival that it was time to act."

"Why?" Seikei could hardly believe all this.

"What did the emperor say to you?" Reigen asked. "Did he agree to resume his duties?"

"No. He told me to find the Kusanagi scroll. Then I would understand."

"Yes," Reigen said softly. "The Kusanagi scroll. Of course he must have read that. But I suppose you couldn't obtain it. The Ministers of the Right and Left wouldn't permit you to see it."

"I *did* find it," Seikei said. He felt an urge to prove to Reigen that he wasn't completely helpless.

"You did?"

"Hato is carrying it right now."

This time, Reigen actually laughed. It was short, however, and immediately he put his hand to his chest as if he had hurt himself. "Well," Reigen said, "you're apparently more resourceful than you look."

"I suppose *you've* read it," Seikei said.

"As a matter of fact, I have," Reigen replied.

Seikei didn't want to ask, but he had to know. "What does it mean? I don't understand why it would make the emperor think he wasn't the emperor."

"Oh, it wasn't the scroll that made him think that," Reigen replied. "The scroll has another message."

"What is it?"

"It told him what he must do to *become* the emperor."

14 — Seikei's New Sword

Hato proved how valuable she was when morning came. She was the first person in the line for breakfast, and brought strong tea and the freshest rice cakes to Reigen and Seikei.

When Hato was returning the empty teacups, Reigen said to Seikei, "You have done your duty. There is no need for you to do any more. Go back to the shogun and tell him the problem will soon be solved. He has other matters he should worry about."

"What other matters?" Seikei asked.

Reigen shrugged. "If Yabuta really has eyes everywhere, he should have informed the shogun of those other matters by now."

"But the emperor—"

"I will find the emperor and I will make him understand he must perform his duties."

"You will? But how?"

"That does not concern you. All that you need care about is that I will do it."

Seikei thought. He knew too little about Reigen. It was still possible that the old man had been involved in the emperor's disappearance. After all, when Seikei left the monastery, he was still there. Even if Reigen was sincere in his wish to restore the emperor to his rightful place, he was only one man. It was possible that Seikei could somehow be useful to him. And certainly, to return to Edo now would be an admission of failure. Seikei could not save his honor by leaving someone else to do the task assigned to him.

"I must continue on the path I have chosen," Seikei told Reigen.

"It will be dangerous," Reigen said. "If you are killed, don't come complaining to me."

"If I am killed . . . ," Seikei began, and then realized this was Reigen's idea of a joke.

"It will be dangerous for your servant as well," said Reigen.

"I will send her away," Seikei replied.

Easier said than done. "Oh, I *see*," Hato said when Seikei told her she could come no farther. "I'm good enough to nurse you back to health, and fetch food for you, but now you think you have no more use for me, bye-bye Hato. After I left my job to serve you? I will have no way to support myself except to beg. This is my reward for loyalty." She broke into tears.

Seikei turned helplessly to Reigen, who shrugged. "Better to let her come along until something frightens her," Reigen said.

Despite her tears, Hato overheard. "I may not be a kami," she said, "but I will remain as true to the emperor as you are."

Suddenly Reigen understood. He pointed at Seikei. "*He* is not the emperor," he said.

"Ha," replied Hato. "Now you're just trying to trick me."

"No, really—" Seikei added, but she cut him off.

"Don't you think I saw that when you clapped your hands, *he* came to rescue you?" Hato said, nodding in Reigen's direction. "Do you think kami appear for just anyone?"

"He's not a kami," said Seikei. He looked at Reigen. "Are you?"

Reigen pursed his lips. For some reason, he gave no answer.

Hato threw up her hands. "That's good enough for me," she said. She gave Seikei a serious look. "There was a rumor in Kyoto, you know, that you have abandoned your duties. When I found you, I knew that you must be on some kind of quest. I wished only to come along, to serve you. I do not care where we are going, or what dangers we may face. I pledged to keep your secret, and I have. How can you send me away now?"

Seikei looked at Reigen. "You can't," Reigen said. "Let's be off."

The road was more crowded today. As they drew closer to Nagoya, they saw more pilgrims heading for the Atsuta Shrine. It was one of the holiest places in the land. Some thought it was second only to the great shrine of Amaterasu at Ise. Seikei had told Hato to leave the Kusanagi scroll as an offering at the monastery, but he wondered if it might have been better to present it at the Atsuta Shrine.

In addition, several more groups of mounted samurai passed the travelers during the day. All of them, Seikei saw, wore the entwined-shrimp emblem that belonged to Lord Ponzu.

Reigen noticed them too. "We may have to defend ourselves once we reach Nagoya," he told Seikei. "Did the shogun send you here with no weapons?"

"I had to leave my swords in Kyoto," Seikei said. He was too ashamed to admit what he really did with them.

Reigen pointed to a wooded area next to the road. "We'll go in there," he said.

Hato followed, because she suspected they were trying to give her the slip. The ground was thick with fallen leaves. Some of them still retained their color; most were brown and brittle. Only a few of the brightest ones still clung stubbornly to the branches of the trees overhead.

Reigen walked deeper into the forest than Seikei thought necessary and it made him uneasy. By now they were long out of sight of the road. Their footsteps crushed some of the dried leaves, making a crackling sound, but otherwise the woods were eerily silent. If Reigen wished to kill them, now would be—

"What are you looking for?" Hato's voice cut through the stillness so unexpectedly that Seikei nearly jumped.

Reigen motioned for her to be silent. He was concentrating on one tree in particular—a maple that still held a few of its bright red leaves high above. Reigen put his hand on the trunk and closed his eyes.

As Seikei watched, Reigen's hand tightened around the tree. His wrinkled skin almost seemed to become part of the rippled bark.

Then there was a crash on the ground behind them. Seikei *did* jump this time, and turned to look, his heart pounding.

A thick branch had fallen from the tree. Of course there were dry branches on the ground throughout the woods. But as Seikei bent to examine this one, he saw that the wood was still green. He looked up and saw the white scar where it had broken off the tree. There seemed to be no reason why it should have fallen.

Reigen picked up the branch and plucked a few small offshoots and red leaves from it. He held it straight out, grasping it at one end. "This will need a little work," he said, "but it should make a fine wooden sword for you."

Seikei saw Hato giving him a look that plainly said, "I told you so."

After building a fire in a clearing in the forest, Reigen carefully stripped the bark from the maple branch. Then he started to shape it, first heating it in the flames, then bending it into a gentle curve. While Hato gathered dry sticks and branches to keep the fire burning, Reigen asked Seikei, "Do you understand where we are going and what we must do?"

"I suppose we are going to the Atsuta Shrine," Seikei said.

Reigen nodded.

"And we are"—Seikei swallowed hard, because this seemed like such a daring thing to say—"going to steal the sword called Kusanagi."

"No," Reigen said firmly. Seikei gave a sigh of relief.

"The sword is too powerful for anyone to possess," Reigen continued. "That was why it was placed in the shrine after Prince Yamato finished conquering all the land under Heaven. Since then, the nation has enjoyed the benefits of peace. If the sword is removed from the shrine, war between the daimyos may break out. Disorder may follow."

Reigen placed one end of the branch into the fire. As Seikei watched, splinters of it burst into flame, then disappeared. The old man withdrew the branch and wiped it with a handful of leaves.

"What we must do," Reigen said without looking up, "is rescue the emperor before anyone else can take the sword."

"But if the emperor wants the sword . . . ," Seikei began.

"He is confused," Reigen said. "I will enlighten him."

"*Someone* must have taken him from the monastery," Seikei pointed out. "Do you know who that could be?"

"I have an idea," Reigen said. "Don't concern yourself with that. Regard anyone who stands in our way as an enemy."

"How will you rescue the emperor?" Seikei asked.

"I cannot predict the future," Reigen said. Hato brought some more firewood and Reigen added it to the flames. When the fire was burning nicely, Reigen ran the entire branch through it from one end to the other. Once more he smoothed and polished it with dried leaves.

He held it out to Seikei. "Use it honorably," he said.

Seikei tested it for weight and balance. He was surprised at how good it felt in his hand. Though it would not cut anyone, it would be useful in a fight. The first time he had ever helped the judge solve a case, Seikei had only a wooden sword. Somehow this one felt even better.

15 — Gathering Ginkgo Nuts

Resuming their journey, the three of them came to a small village where people made a living selling food and other supplies to travelers. Seikei smelled something that seemed familiar, but he could not at first identify it.

"Ginkgo porridge," said Hato, pointing to a stand where it was sold.

The woman who made the porridge ladled out each portion with a smile that showed she had few teeth. Seikei tasted the thick, hot liquid, finding that it was nearly as good as the porridge his mother had made when he was a child. "Do you recall a boy about my age having a bowl of your porridge in the past two or three days?" he asked the woman.

"Oh, many people come by here," she replied. "Men, women, boys, girls. Everybody likes my porridge."

Seikei nodded. "This boy . . . would have particularly liked it. Maybe he even had more than one bowl."

The woman cocked her head to one side. "Now that you mention it, there *was* such a boy. I thought maybe he hadn't eaten in days. He ate *four* bowls of porridge. Can you imagine? Even *I* don't like my porridge that much."

"Was anybody with him?"

"Five men. Samurai. They were pretty impatient, I recall. Very amazed that this boy wanted to eat porridge and eat more porridge. Who do you think he was, making them wait like that? Daimyo's son or something?"

Seikei glanced at Reigen, who had been listening. Reigen asked the woman, "Do you recall the crest that the samurai wore on their garments?"

"Oh, I'm pretty sure it was Lord Ponzu's crest," she said. "A lot of his men have passed along the road lately."

"Yes," said Reigen. "I noticed that too."

So had Seikei, and he was almost afraid to think what it meant.

When they had moved on, Reigen asked, "How did you know he liked ginkgo porridge?"

"He ate two bowls of it while I was at the monastery," said Seikei. "One of them was mine."

Hato hadn't missed any of this. "So that means," she said, "that the person you are pursuing on your quest is only a boy?"

"Yes," said Seikei.

She seemed disappointed. "I was hoping it would be a monster," she said. "Like the ones heroes slay in stories. I've never seen a monster. Or at least a dragon. Don't heroes usually destroy something that terrifies people?"

"If you are bored, perhaps you should go home," suggested Reigen.

"You won't get rid of me that easily," Hato replied.

"I thought not," muttered Reigen through his teeth.

"Besides," Hato continued, "now I can be a great help to you. Other than being the emperor's faithful servant, I mean."

"How?" asked Seikei.

"If the person you want to capture likes ginkgo porridge, I can make some," she said. "Mine is much better than the kind that woman back there sells."

Reigen was silent for a moment before saying, "In that way, you could possibly be helpful."

Unfortunately, their progress slowed after that, because whenever they passed a ginkgo tree, Hato wanted to gather nuts. Worse yet, the nuts smelled bad—so bad that Seikei and Reigen didn't want to walk too close to Hato after she collected some.

"It's only the soft outer covering that stinks," said Hato. "It will soon fall off. The nut itself is very mild."

As Hato hurried ahead of them, Seikei asked Reigen,

"What do you think Lord Ponzu's men plan to do with . . . the emperor?"

"For now, it is safer not to call him that," said Reigen. "As you know Yabuta has eyes—and ears—everywhere."

"His name in the monastery was Risu," said Seikei.

"Squirrel?"

"Because he was so fond of . . ." Seikei gestured toward Hato, bending over to pick up more ginkgo nuts.

"I see. Let us call him that. Lord Ponzu's men are clearly going to take him to their daimyo's castle, which is in Nagoya as well. That is no doubt why Lord Ponzu heard of the sword and the legend attached to it."

"Is it only a legend?" asked Seikei.

"Legends can be powerful," said Reigen. "They can also be a way of expressing the truth."

"So . . . do you think Lord Ponzu is planning a revolt to overthrow the shogun?"

"That could well be his intention," said Reigen. "With the emperor at the head of his troops, in possession of the Kusanagi, he could not be defeated."

"But many people will be killed."

"Yes," said Reigen. "That is the nature of war. Those who suffer most will be those who are least able to defend themselves. The farmers, the shopkeepers, people like those." Reigen gestured toward a group of pilgrims who kept gawking at the sights around them. For those who had never before left the villages in which they had been born, each stage of the road offered a new wonder.

"Why would Lord Ponzu want to disturb harmony and cause so much misery?" Seikei asked.

"It is *his* nature," said Reigen. "Some men, whether great lords or small, are satisfied with the land they have been entrusted with. Others look with envy at their neighbor's land and covet that. But then, even if they are able to take their neighbor's domain, now someone *else's* land is next to theirs. They must move on until they possess all the land—or until someone stronger stops them."

"The shogun is stronger than Lord Ponzu," Seikei said. He hoped that was true. But even so, Seikei's failure to report the story the ronin told him looked more serious than ever.

"Not if Lord Ponzu has the emperor—and the sword—on his side," Reigen said.

Hato came running up, her arms full of ginkgo nuts. The smell was overpowering, but she didn't seem to notice. Reigen tied the nuts into a piece of cloth, but made Hato carry it.

As they proceeded on toward Nagoya, Reigen said, "This Yabuta, if he has eyes everyplace, must know of Lord Ponzu's intentions."

"Yes," said Seikei. "He does."

"We must be watchful of him."

"Why? He wants the same thing we do," said Seikei.

"Not necessarily," replied Reigen. He stopped, shaded his eyes, and looked down the road. "Tell me what you see there," he said.

Seikei peered into the distance. A line of people had formed. "Samurai are stopping travelers to check their luggage," he told Reigen.

"Whose samurai?"

Even from here, Seikei easily recognized the shogun's crest. "It's all right," he said. "They are the shogun's samurai, not Lord Ponzu's, and we no longer have the scroll." He was glad now that they had left it at the monastery.

"It's *not* all right," said Reigen. "They are looking for the person who stole the sacred mirror from the Purple Hall at the palace."

Seikei was amazed. "How do you know this?"

"Because I am the one who took it."

16 — AN OLD "FRIEND"

"Why would you—" Seikei started to ask.

"Never mind," said Reigen. "I must leave you now. Go into Nagoya and find out whatever you can at Lord Ponzu's castle. I will see you tomorrow or the following day at the Atsuta Shrine."

Seikei nodded. "But what are you going to do?"

He was already talking to Reigen's back. Showing surprising agility, the old man had left the road and was hopping from rock to rock on a muddy slope that led downhill toward Lake Biwa. Seikei couldn't imagine how he planned to get to Nagoya that way, but Reigen had shown that he was resourceful. Seikei's new sword was testimony to that.

He and Hato passed through the checkpoint and not long afterward reached Nagoya. It was not difficult to find Lord Ponzu's castle. Five stories high, it towered over the southern part of the city. Guards in each of its four towers glared down at those who approached.

"It will be almost impossible to rescue him from there," Seikei said.

"You've already forgotten my plan," said Hato. "I will offer these ginkgo nuts at the kitchen. If the boy you are seeking likes porridge all that much, the cooks will certainly need the nuts. Then I'll ask for a job. I'm really very useful, even though *you* may not have noticed."

"Supposing that works—" Seikei started to say.

"I'll find out where they're keeping this boy. What's his name?"

Seikei hesitated. "The last time I saw him, his name was Risu."

"But he might be in disguise now," she added. "I understand. Well, I'll sneak in to see him, and tell him that the emperor is waiting for him. Then we'll slip away—"

"No, no, no," Seikei said. "Don't tell him that."

"Why not?"

"Well . . . suppose he doesn't believe you."

"Even if he doesn't," Hato said, "it ought to make him curious!"

Seikei nodded. "Yes, I'm very sure that it would. But you must remember your pledge to me. Don't tell anyone I am the emperor."

"Oh, all right," she said, "but you're making things unnecessarily difficult."

"I have my reasons," he said, hoping she wouldn't ask what they were.

"Well, I'll find *some* way to get him out. Then will you be waiting right here?"

"No." Seikei strongly doubted that Hato would even get to see the emperor, much less take him out of the castle. But perhaps she could find out something useful. "Listen," he said. "Tomorrow at this same time, whether you have Risu or not, come outside. I'll try to meet you."

"And if you aren't here?"

"Go to the Atsuta Shrine. Reigen promised to be there."

"All right." She bowed very low before Seikei, making him look around to check if people were watching.

"Don't do that again," he said.

"I promise," she replied. "Until we're safely back at your palace."

"Yes," Seikei said. "At the palace that will be fine. Not elsewhere."

"Good-bye, chrysanthemum boy," Hato said with a wink. She turned and headed for the castle gate. Seikei breathed a sigh of relief, and set out to find the shrine.

People were happy to give him directions, but it was

unnecessary. All he had to do was follow the crowd of pilgrims who were carrying gifts they had brought as offerings. It was like stepping into a river of people that would sweep him to his destination.

Before he even came in sight of the shrine, however, the crowd stopped moving. People milled about and soon the entire street was filled from one side to the other. Everyone was asking what the reason for the delay was.

Then the answer came, creating a buzz through the crowd like a swarm of bees, growing louder each moment. "They've closed the shrine! The priests have closed the shrine." At first this was said with dismay, but then a growing anger crept into the voices. Most of these people had come long distances at a great sacrifice. For some, it was the only such journey they would make in a lifetime. To be stopped just short of their goal was almost intolerable.

Now new questions began circulating: "Why is the shrine closed?"

"How long will it be closed? Who can tell us?"

"Well, young sir, I never expected to see you again."

Seikei had been listening to the questions from the crowd, and it took a moment before he realized the comment was directed at him.

He turned, and there stood the ronin Takanori. Now,

however, he wore a crisp new silk kimono, decorated with the hollyhock crest worn by the shogun's men. Seikei's first emotion was anger, because here was the person who had caused him all this trouble.

Then he realized he should beware, for if Takanori was here, Yabuta must be nearby. He searched the crowd with his eyes, but saw only groups of upset pilgrims.

"Looking for someone?" asked Takanori.

"The person you serve now," Seikei replied.

"I serve the shogun now," Takanori said with an air of self-righteousness that grated on Seikei. "As you once did."

"I still serve him," Seikei said angrily.

"Not wisely or well," Takanori commented. "After Yabuta found that you did not commit seppuku, he told me you would come here. I did not think you were that foolish, but Yabuta knew. He knows everything."

"So he sent you to find me?" Seikei said. "What are you supposed to do now?" His hand went to the hilt of his sword and this time he had the satisfaction of finding it. Though it was only a wooden one, he was willing to test it against Takanori's steel blades.

Takanori saw the gesture. He said, "I could kill you right here if I wished." He was merely pointing out something Seikei should know, not threatening him.

"Why haven't you, then?" asked Seikei.

"Yabuta wishes to meet you, to talk with you," Takanori replied.

"What about?"

"Come with me and you will find out."

"I'm not going to commit seppuku," said Seikei. "No matter what he says."

"He knows that," said Takanori.

Seikei considered the offer. Right now it seemed impossible for him to get to the shrine. Reigen probably wouldn't be there yet anyway. Seikei had to admit he was curious about what Yabuta had to say. But would Yabuta want information? He would certainly use torture if he thought it would loosen Seikei's tongue.

On the other hand, Seikei knew nothing important that Yabuta didn't already know. Yabuta wouldn't know or care about Hato. Or Reigen? What did Seikei know about Reigen? Really, nothing except that he had taken the sacred mirror from the palace. There was no need to tell Yabuta about that.

Seikei decided. "Do we have far to go?" he asked Takanori.

They didn't. Takanori led him down a side street to avoid the crowds. As far as Seikei could tell, they circled through the city to a place on the other side of the shrine. Takanori took him to a nondescript shop with no sign to indicate what it sold. As soon as they stepped onto the porch, however, the door opened. Another samurai stood there, looking as if he would swiftly turn away anyone who did not belong.

Takanori and Seikei passed the guard's inspection and entered. They were in an empty hallway, so bleak that the building almost seemed deserted. Then Seikei caught a whiff of something in the air. He took a second breath. There was no doubt what it was.

Blood. Dried now, not fresh. But there had been bloodshed in this place at some time past.

Seikei could feel fear starting to overcome him, and he fought against it. If the next blood to be spilled here was his, he would bear it as a samurai should. For death, he reminded himself, comes to all. The only way to meet it is with courage.

17 — A Robe for Seikei

Takanori took Seikei to a small room in the rear of the building. The smell was stronger here. If anyone screamed, Seikei thought, they would not be heard by passersby in the street.

When the door opened, there sat Yabuta. His eyes still blazed with the hatred he had shown for Seikei earlier, but he spoke in a softer tone. "I am glad you have chosen to come here willingly," he said. "Sit down."

Seikei sat on a mat facing him. Takanori slid the door shut, but stood behind Seikei as if Yabuta might need him.

"My curiosity was aroused when I learned that you had chosen to live, not die," Yabuta began. "I wondered what your plans were." He looked at Seikei's obi, where only a wooden sword now rested. "Without your swords,"

Yabuta pointed out, "you cannot return to Edo. Judge Ooka would be dishonored."

"I intend to regain my swords," Seikei said. "I left them in a safe place," he added, wondering if Yabuta knew exactly what he had done with them.

"That may be possible," said Yabuta. "It may even be possible for me to forget all the errors you committed on the way to Kyoto." Seikei realized that Yabuta was attempting to be friendly. The effect was chilling, as if a snake were trying to act like a playful dog.

"How could that happen?" asked Seikei.

"Tell me what brings you to Nagoya," Yabuta replied, as though he wanted to show Seikei the sights.

Seikei hesitated. "You must know already," he said, "since you sent Takanori to meet me."

"The shrine," Yabuta said, nodding. "And if you were going to the shrine, you must know what it contains."

"The Kusanagi," Seikei replied. "The sword that cut the burning grass."

Yabuta smiled, as if he and Seikei thought alike. "Very good. I suppose it was you who left the Kusanagi scroll at the Buddhist monastery on the Tokaido Road."

Seikei nodded. He decided it was wise not to mention Hato's role.

"Do you know how important that sword is?" asked Yabuta.

Seikei considered the question carefully. "I know it is very powerful."

"So what did you think you would do if you reached the shrine?" Yabuta asked. "Take the sword? No one but the priests is even permitted to see it."

"I . . . I didn't set out to get the sword," Seikei said. "I hoped to find the emperor here."

Yabuta looked slightly disappointed. "You don't understand the significance of the sword at all, do you?" he asked Seikei.

No, Seikei admitted to himself. Reigen had told him that the sword could make Risu become the emperor. But how?

Yabuta leaned closer, as if he were confiding an important secret. "Lord Ponzu has taken the emperor," he explained. "I have only a few men at my disposal, not enough to storm Lord Ponzu's castle and rescue him." He looked at Seikei. "Do you know what this means?"

Seikei shook his head.

"If Lord Ponzu succeeds in putting the sword into the emperor's hands, he can overthrow the shogun."

"Because he who possesses the sword is all-powerful?" said Seikei, remembering what Reigen had told him.

"Because people will *believe* the legend of the sword," Yabuta said. "If they believe the emperor cannot be defeated, they will not resist him."

"I . . . I don't think the emperor even *wants* to overthrow the shogun," said Seikei.

"Of course he doesn't," Yabuta hissed, as if Seikei were a particularly slow-witted schoolboy. "He is only Lord Ponzu's tool. Lord Ponzu is the one with ambition. He wishes to put himself in the place of the shogun. Afterward, he will allow the emperor to resume his useless existence as a figurehead living in luxury."

Seikei nodded slowly, though he still had misgivings. Risu had said very definitely that he wasn't the emperor, and if he wanted to live in luxury, why did he leave the palace in the first place?

"You can redeem yourself," said Yabuta in a silky tone.

Seikei was wary. "What do you want me to do?"

"Nothing difficult at all," Yabuta replied. "And in return, I will forget all the disgraceful things you have done. You can return to Edo, just as if you had fulfilled your mission."

Seikei waited. He suspected Yabuta would not be so generous unless he wanted Seikei to do something exceedingly dangerous or hideously dishonorable.

"I want you to take the sword," said Yabuta.

"But you just said no one but the priests—" Seikei protested.

"The priests, and, naturally, the emperor," Yabuta said smoothly.

"Then how can I—oh, no," Seikei said, understanding what Yabuta intended.

"Fortunately, few people ever *see* the emperor," Yabuta said, ignoring Seikei's look. "I happen to know that he has never visited the Atsuta Shrine. The priests who administer the shrine know only that he is a boy about your age."

"Even so," said Seikei, "they must have some way to . . . to determine if . . ." He trailed off, because Yabuta had signaled Takanori to bring someone else into the room. Seikei turned and saw the Ministers of the Right and Left. Their haughty looks had disappeared. Now they eyed Yabuta fearfully, as if he were some sort of dangerous beast that had broken into the house.

"Do you have the robe the emperor wears when he makes a formal visit to a shrine?" Yabuta asked them.

"We brought the one he wore when he went to Ise," the Minister of the Right said.

"But of course the Atsuta Shrine is less important," said the Minister of the Left. "So that robe may be regarded as—"

“Put the robe on him,” said Yabuta, pointing to Seikei.

The two ministers looked as if he had told them to dress a dog in the emperor’s robe. One of them tried to stammer out an objection, but Yabuta said, “I really only need one of you. If I decide which one is less helpful, I won’t have to tolerate this chatter any longer. Because a severed head cannot speak.”

The ministers hurried to accomplish their task. Seikei let them, not knowing what else to do.

After he was dressed, he understood at least one reason why he wouldn’t want to be emperor. The robe was bulky and quite heavy. It included tight undergarments that added to his discomfort. The outfit was topped off by a high hat that covered Seikei’s commoner haircut and even the hachimaki headband. Finally the ministers slipped sandals with high soles on his feet, making him seem taller, but also making it nearly impossible to walk.

“That doesn’t matter,” said Yabuta when Seikei pointed this out. “The ministers will be carrying you in a *kago.*”

The ministers opened their mouths in unison, but seeing Yabuta’s look, carefully shut them again—silently.

18 – The Secret of the Shrine

Seikei recalled the last time he had ridden in a kago. He and his father the tea merchant were traveling on the Tokaido Road. Father believed in comfort, telling Seikei it was one of the benefits gained from earning money. Yet even though Seikei had ridden in a cushioned box carried by two burly men, he had yearned to be walking.

Here he was again, though the imperial ministers were frailer than professional kago-bearers. The kago itself was much more luxurious than the one Seikei had used before. Even so, he still wanted to be one of the ordinary pilgrims who surrounded the shrine, demanding to know why they were not allowed entry. It was, of course, Yabuta who had ordered the shrine closed.

Despite the crush of the crowd, the ministers had no

trouble getting through. Peeking through a slit in the front of the kago, Seikei saw why. Yabuta's men—several tall samurai wearing the shogun's crest—were marching ahead of them. If people didn't move out of the way fast enough, the samurai used clubs to hurry them. Takanori and two others brought up the rear. That was a good idea, for when word spread that the emperor himself was in the kago, the throng of pilgrims pressed toward it. They ignored the blows of the samurai, stretching their hands out, trying to touch the kago. They believed that the emperor, as a living kami, had the power to heal whatever afflicted them.

Yabuta had been at the head of the procession and for a while seemed to be swallowed up by the crowd. Seikei momentarily hoped that he had met one of Lord Ponzu's samurai and been struck down. Then he reminded himself that Ponzu was an enemy of the shogun. However ruthless Yabuta seemed to be, Seikei should be glad to help him foil Lord Ponzu's rebellion.

Yet Reigen's cautionary words kept echoing through Seikei's mind. When Seikei had said that Yabuta had wanted the same thing they did—to rescue the emperor—Reigen had replied, "Not necessarily." And Reigen had also warned him that the Kusanagi sword was too powerful for anyone to possess. In a short time, if all went well, Seikei would be holding it in his hands. What would happen then? The words of the Kusanagi scroll came into his mind: *Prince Yamato placed a spell on it to make sure that only a descendant of Amaterasu would have the ability to remove it from its resting place.*

Of course, Yabuta would say that was only a legend.

Something jolted the kago, knocking Seikei against the side of the box. He looked and saw that the press of the crowd had nearly caused one of the ministers to fall. If the kago crashed to the ground and broke open, it might throw the pilgrims into such a frenzy that they would tear Seikei apart in their desire to touch him.

Seikei thought wryly that if that happened, Hato would never be convinced he hadn't been the emperor. On the other hand, it would be more like her to show up at the shrine with the *real* emperor just as Seikei arrived. Even Yabuta would have a hard time explaining that.

No, Seikei told himself. That couldn't happen if Hato followed his instructions. She was only supposed to come to the shrine *tomorrow,* unless Seikei met her outside Lord Ponzu's castle first.

He heard cries of pain from outside the kago. Peering

through the crack he saw Yabuta's men roughly shoving people out of the way; some were being trampled by others pressing forward. Seikei felt trapped, like a duck kept in a wooden cage at the marketplace, whose only fate was to be taken to someone's home and eaten. It would be impossible for him to flee, even if he opened the kago door and jumped out.

Finally they reached the torii gate. Seikei clapped his hands with a silent prayer to the kami of the shrine. *Help me preserve my honor by doing what is right.*

The priests of the shrine were waiting for them. One let down the *simenawa,* or sacred rope across the entrance, that had barred the pilgrims from entering. Yabuta's men kept the crowd at bay as the ministers carried the kago inside. Then the rope was put in place again.

No rope could have restrained the pilgrims if Seikei emerged from the kago in full view of the street. So the two ministers, by now breathing heavily with the exertion, had to lug Seikei and the kago up the steps and inside the *haiden,* the worship hall of the shrine. He felt them gently set the kago down on the wooden floor. Realizing that, as the emperor, it was beneath his dignity to open the kago door himself, he waited.

Sure enough, presently it slid aside and Seikei

peered out. The room seemed full of Shinto priests, most in white robes. Four of them, closest to the kago, immediately knelt, followed almost at once by four behind them. Like ripples through a pond, several more rows of monks knelt in turn. In the very last row, however, one man, dressed the same as the others, remained standing.

Seikei saw who it was: Reigen. He froze as the old man's eyes locked on his. The look on Reigen's face was not one of approval; he looked very much as he had when Lord Ponzu's men had passed by on the road. Seikei waited for him to announce, "That's not the emperor." But instead, Reigen merely slipped silently aside, out of Seikei's view.

The other priests remained kneeling, motionless, for what seemed like too long a time. Seikei wondered if they were waiting for *him* to do something. He decided that Yabuta would have let him know if that were necessary.

Trying not to make it seem obvious, Seikei leaned forward. He wanted to see where Reigen had gone. What would the old man do? If he reported what he knew to Yabuta or the two ministers, of course it wouldn't matter. But there must be a chief priest in charge of the shrine.

In order to assume a priestly identity and robes, Reigen must know him well. If at that very moment Reigen was telling him that the boy in the kago was a fraud, that would explain the delay.

The sound of a small bell abruptly broke the silence. It seemed to be a signal, for the kneeling priests visibly relaxed. Some even looked up, although Seikei noticed that none were so bold as to look directly at him.

The two ministers appeared on either side of the kago doorway. They reached for Seikei's hands, and he allowed them to help him out of the kago. He didn't have to walk, fortunately, because two priests appeared, carrying a wooden chair.

The chair had no decorations on it. It was made of plain, unpainted wooden planks fitted together. The wood was worn and pitted, clearly very old, perhaps dating back hundreds of years. Very reluctantly, Seikei sat down, for he knew that those who had used the chair before him must have been far more worthy than he.

One of the ministers put a flat wooden sceptre in his hand, whispering, "Hold it upright during the ceremony." Seikei sighed, but did as he was told.

After he was settled, four young priests raised the chair on their shoulders and placed it on a high platform. From here Seikei could look down on everyone in the hall. He strained his eyes to locate Reigen, but could not find him. He noticed that although Yabuta and the two ministers had entered the haiden, none of the samurai Yabuta had brought were permitted inside. This was a sacred place.

Music now began, accompanied by chanting that Seikei barely understood. He recognized it as the same ancient language that had been used for the scroll. He could make out a few words of praise and prayers for the emperor's long life.

Seikei was embarrassed. Any kami who inhabited this shrine must be thoroughly disgusted with the fraud. Seikei looked at the high ceiling, wondering if Susanoo might put a bolt of lightning through it to bring the ceremony to a halt.

No one but Seikei seemed concerned, however, and the music continued. It was not the lively kind of music that had been performed at *kabuki* plays Seikei had seen. Instead it was solemn and slow.

Quite slow, and seemingly never-ending. Seikei found it difficult to hold the sceptre upright for so long. He wondered if it would be acceptable to shift it to his other hand. Better not, he told himself.

Dancers appeared—a line of young women who encircled the platform Seikei's chair rested on. The women were pretty, but none of them smiled. Keeping time to the music, they moved slowly and danced as if they were carrying heavy weights.

At last, the music changed. It became a little faster, as if preparing for something important to happen. Seikei tried to conceal his relief as the young priests lifted him down from the platform. All around him, the temple dancers had fallen to the floor, resting there as motionless as if they had been autumn leaves.

The oldest of the priests in the hall stepped forward and stood beside Seikei. He wore a purple garment, indicating his high rank. He gave a signal, and someone opened the door that led from this part of the shrine to the inner honden. In there, Seikei knew, the sacred objects inhabited by the kami were preserved. Seikei had never even seen the inside of a honden before, much less been there. Now it was clear he was supposed to enter.

"He'll show you the resting place of the sword," one of the ministers whispered in his ear. "You will have to open the box and remove it."

The other minister bent to remove Seikei's high-soled

sandals. He left on the white cotton *tabi* socks, and Seikei stepped forward. The wooden floor was rough, and there was no danger of him slipping. At the moment he entered the honden, the music behind him stopped. A hush fell over the hall. Seikei sensed, rather than heard, the old priest follow him.

The honden was nearly dark; a little light came from high above, where there was an open space in the roof. As his eyes grew accustomed to the darkness, Seikei saw a long, shiny black lacquered box resting on a low table in the center of the room. He assumed this must be the repository of the sword. His palms grew cold at the thought of having to lift it.

Moving closer, he saw that the lid of the box was slightly off center. He waited until the high priest caught up with him, because Seikei felt he needed a witness.

He glanced at the priest to see if there was to be any further ceremony before the lid was removed. Evidently not, for the old man seemed to be waiting for *him.*

Seikei touched the lid, half expecting to be struck dead for doing what only Amaterasu's living descendant should do. He put his fingers under it, finding that it wasn't heavy. A scent like faint perfume reached his nostrils from the inside of the box. He lifted the lid and looked down.

The high priest made a sound, something like a squeak, and took a step back. Seikei thought for a moment that the man would fall.

The box was empty. The Kusanagi was gone.

19 — The Ronin's Surprise

Seikei feared that the priests of the shrine would draw the obvious conclusion. Since the sword had left the shrine, it stood to reason that the person who came to claim it was an impostor.

That didn't happen. When the chief priest emerged from the honden, he announced the loss of the sword in a voice that trembled with fear and shame. Everyone looked at Seikei. He suddenly realized that they expected him to be angry. The custodians of the shrine, whose primary duty had been to protect and preserve the Kusanagi, had failed.

Seikei tried to play the part by looking stern. That succeeded so well that all the priests, the musicians, and the shrine dancers fell to their knees, bowing their heads.

Leaving only three people besides Seikei standing: the two ministers, who looked fearful, and Yabuta, who did not. In fact, Yabuta looked exactly the way Seikei, as the emperor, was supposed to feel.

Yabuta stared at Seikei with such rage that Seikei felt it like a blast of hot air. He expected Yabuta to denounce him immediately and order his death. In fact, Seikei thought he would be lucky if death was all that Yabuta had in store for him.

But that didn't happen either. Instead, Yabuta abruptly turned and stalked out of the haiden. Evidently he had decided on some other course of action.

The two ministers looked helplessly at Seikei. Seikei understood. Since they had brought him here as the emperor, it was impossible for them to abandon that deception. There was only one way to get out of here.

Seikei pointed to his sandals, left on the floor outside the honden. One of the ministers slipped them back onto Seikei's feet, and Seikei stepped into the kago.

The door slid shut, and Seikei felt the ministers lift him off the floor. He regretted leaving the shrine without a final word for the priests, but "Don't worry. It's not your fault," seemed unlike anything an emperor would say.

Seikei worried about how the ministers were going to get through the crowd outside without Yabuta and his men. But Takanori was waiting for the kago at the shrine gate. "Make way!" he shouted. "The kago is empty. The emperor has remained at the shrine. Let us through."

Seikei had to admire this strategy. Except for a few people who wanted just to touch the empty kago, the crowd moved aside. It did not take long before they arrived back at the house where Seikei had met Yabuta. The ministers set the kago down much less gently than when they had carried the "emperor." Seikei had to open the kago door himself.

This time, no one knelt on seeing him. He faced Takanori, who stood ready to draw his sword. "Take off that costume," he told Seikei, "and leave it in the kago."

Seikei did as he was told, keeping only the undergarments. Takanori took him inside the house. Once more Seikei noticed the smell of blood. This time he was certain his own blood would soon be mingled with it. He could think of no reason why Yabuta would want him to live, and several why Yabuta would want him dead.

The two ministers had disappeared. Takanori showed no interest in them. He slid open the door to a room and motioned Seikei inside. "Sit," Takanori said, and Seikei took a seat on the matted floor. He looked around, but saw no bloodstains. If he were going to kill someone, he would choose a room where there would be no mats that would need to be burned later.

The house seemed utterly empty. Takanori stood vigilant, with his back against the wooden-frame wall, but said nothing. The paper between the frames was plain brown, with no decorations. Seikei thought he had never been in so dull a room.

"What are you waiting for?" Seikei asked finally. He noticed that his voice shook, and chided himself for it.

"I am waiting for Yabuta," said Takanori. "Or someone bringing orders from him."

Seikei could see that Takanori relished the power he held. Seikei wanted to puncture his self-assurance. "Suppose Yabuta has abandoned you," he suggested.

"He would never do that," Takanori replied. "I have been too useful to him."

"Just because you told him that story about Lord Ponzu?" Seikei scoffed. "And revealed that you had told me the same thing earlier?"

Takanori gave Seikei an unpleasant smile. "You never figured that out, did you? It was Yabuta who *sent* me to meet you on the road and tell you that story."

Seikei couldn't keep the surprise from showing on his face. "But then . . . the story was false all along?"

"Oh, no," Takanori said, delighted with the effect his words were having. "Lord Ponzu really is planning a rebellion against the shogun. Yabuta encouraged him to do so."

"Encouraged him?" Seikei felt as if he were waking from a dream and the world had suddenly become very different from what it had been before.

"Yes," said Takanori. "Oh, Lord Ponzu really is as greedy as I've told you. It required only a few suggestions from Yabuta to persuade him that he could overthrow the shogun. All it would take would be to capture the emperor and take the Kusanagi sword."

"But why would Yabuta do such a thing?" Seikei asked. "He is one of the shogun's officials."

Takanori nodded. "You see how smart he is? Imagine how grateful the shogun will be, how generously he will reward Yabuta, when he learns that the head of the Guards of the Inner Garden has foiled a rebellion."

"Foiled?" Seikei shook his head, as if something were loose inside. "I thought you said he suggested the rebellion."

"Of course," Takanori said. "And thus he would know all of Lord Ponzu's plans. Yabuta even has men loyal to him among Ponzu's forces, ready to act when Yabuta gives the word."

"Traitors? How could anyone be so dishonorable?"

Takanori laughed as if Seikei were a child. "Because when Lord Ponzu is defeated, those who served Yabuta will receive part of the lord's domain." He clasped the hilt of his sword and stood tall. "I will be rewarded that way myself."

"But why did you approach me with the story of Lord Ponzu's rebellion?" Seikei asked. "I could have reported it immediately."

"Yabuta didn't think so," said Takanori. "He told me to make the story unconvincing. He was angry that the shogun trusted you to persuade the emperor to resume his duties. Yabuta feared that that if you succeeded, your father would rise in the shogun's favor. This way, Yabuta could make sure you were disgraced." He paused and shrugged. "Even if you *had* reported the story of the rebellion, Yabuta would simply have called it off, and made you appear to be a fool."

"So it was all my fault," Seikei said miserably.

"Why blame yourself?" asked Takanori. "Yabuta is just much smarter than anyone else. You could still be useful to him, you know."

Seikei was curious enough to ask, "How?"

"Well, even though the sword was already gone, everyone at the shrine accepted you as the emperor. Perhaps Yabuta would want you to continue that role. Then the shogun would have no more trouble getting the emperor to fulfill his duties."

"You've forgotten about the *real* emperor," said Seikei.

"Oh, no," replied Takanori. "Yabuta has already decided what to do with him. When the sword turned out to be missing, you see, Yabuta knew Lord Ponzu must have taken it."

Seikei doubted that. He had a pretty good idea who *had* stolen the sword, but he wasn't about to share that with Takanori.

"That must mean Lord Ponzu has decided not to wait any longer," said Takanori. "So it is time for Yabuta to put down the rebellion."

"How is he going to do that?"

"By setting fire to Ponzu's castle. When the daimyo emerges, Yabuta and his samurai will kill him. And I suspect, to get the emperor out of the way once and for all, Yabuta will do away with him too." He smiled at Seikei. "Of course, Yabuta will need a replacement. If not you, then someone else."

Seikei thought of Hato, who might well be with the emperor at this moment. He had to get out of here, to warn her. To warn them both, he reminded himself. But how?

"I . . . I don't think that will work," he told Takanori.

Before the samurai could respond, a sword popped out of his chest.

Seikei gaped at it, feeling more than ever as if unnatural events were taking place.

Takanori, of course, was equally surprised. Without thinking, he reached down and grasped the blade with both hands. It seemed as if his first thought was to pull it out.

Seikei wanted to tell him that he was doing it wrong. He wouldn't be able to pull it through his body, because it must have a hilt on the unseen side. He should be pushing. But Seikei found himself unable to utter a word. He could only watch in horrified fascination.

The sword was now moving back into Takanori's body, seemingly of its own accord. Takanori's fingers were sliced to shreds as he struggled to hold it.

Finally the sword disappeared, and Takanori held up his bleeding hands as if he saw something approaching and was trying desperately to stop it. Seikei nearly looked over his shoulder to see what it was, but couldn't take his eyes off the ribbons of flesh hanging from the samurai's hands.

The sword, apparently, had been all that was keeping Takanori upright. After it left his body, he fell facedown on the floor. A pool of blood spread rapidly around him. Someone will have to burn those mats now, Seikei thought.

With Takanori no longer blocking his view, Seikei could see clearly what had happened. There was a rip in the paper wall behind where Takanori had been standing. Someone had plunged a sword right through the wall and into his back.

Someone . . . whose shadow Seikei could see moving along the wall.

Someone . . . who then began to slide open the door of the room.

It was the person Seikei most feared seeing: Reigen. He stood in the doorway, wiping the blade of what looked like a very, very old sword.

20 — A Message from Hato

"Is that . . . ," Seikei started to ask.

"Yes," Reigen said, returning the blade to its scabbard. It was now the only sword he carried. He no longer wore monk's robes, but instead a purple kimono with a white chrysanthemum design. "This is the Kusanagi. I had to take it from its resting place to keep it from falling into the *wrong hands.*" He gave Seikei a meaningful look.

Seikei hung his head. "Yabuta told me that I had to take the sword to stop Lord Ponzu's rebellion," he said.

"It does not matter now," said Reigen. "We must go to Lord Ponzu's palace."

Seikei got to his feet, realizing that he wore only the emperor's undergarments and high sandals.

"You can't go like that," said Reigen. "Where is the sword I made for you?"

It didn't take long for Seikei to find his other clothes

and the wooden sword in a nearby room. As he dressed, Reigen said, "There is something I want you to promise."

"I know," said Seikei. "I learned my lesson. Regard anyone who stands in our way as an enemy."

"Yes, but something even more important," said Reigen. "You will not need to use your sword against anyone, as long as I am near. With the Kusanagi, I can defeat any enemies."

Seikei was a little disappointed. He hoped to be of some use, and now it seemed as if Reigen was going to ask him to promise to stay out of the way.

"I want you to remain vigilant at all times," said Reigen. "Be ready to use your sword—on me. Or anyone else who holds the Kusanagi."

Seikei couldn't believe what he heard. "On you? Why?"

"I told you before that the sword is too powerful for anyone to possess. That includes me. I would have left it where it was, had not Yabuta tried to seize it."

"But with the sword, you cannot be defeated," Seikei said. "How could I even attempt to use a wooden sword against you?"

"When I made your sword," replied Reigen, "I gave it the power to defeat me."

"I cannot do what you ask," said Seikei. "How would I know when to do it? Suppose—"

"I will let you know," said Reigen. "Be alert."

Seikei shook his head, thinking of the training sessions Bunzo had put him through. The judge's chief samurai had constantly told him to remain alert, on guard at all times. Seikei had seen Bunzo, apparently asleep, suddenly open his eyes, ready to act, if he heard a strange sound. "I will try," Seikei said. But he secretly felt he would not have the courage to attack Reigen.

Reigen had two horses waiting outside. As they rode toward Lord Ponzu's castle, they saw that it was too late. A plume of smoke was rising above that part of the city. Before reaching the palace, they encountered a swarm of people fleeing from the fire. Many of them carried possessions on their backs. Clearly they were people who lived near the castle, and feared that the fire would spread. Unlike Edo, where the judge had organized fire brigades for each section of the city, Nagoya had no regular fire fighters.

That was obvious as Seikei and Reigen came upon the scene. Behind a high stone wall, the wooden castle was blazing fiercely. Two of its five towers were engulfed already, and looked as if they might collapse at any moment. It would have been nearly impossible to put out the fire at this point, even if a thousand fire fighters with buckets of water had been available. The castle was doomed.

Now Yabuta's plan became clear. There were only three entrances—or exits—in the high stone wall that surrounded the castle grounds. Yabuta's men, along with the traitors among Lord Ponzu's samurai, blocked all three. Seikei could hear the cries of the frightened people on the other side, pleading to be allowed to get away from the raging fire. Seikei could feel the heat of the flames even from a distance.

The emperor was in there, he thought. And Hato, who had been so faithful to him. He wanted to urge his horse forward in an attempt to save them, but of course that would be futile. He looked at Reigen to see what the old man would do.

Reigen was straining his eyes. The smoke and the chaos, with people running past them on all sides, made it difficult even for Seikei to see anything.

Suddenly a chorus of shouts rose above the other noise. It came from the gate nearest to them, and Reigen headed in that direction. Seikei followed.

A battle was going on for control of the gate. Some of the samurai who had remained loyal were attempting to force their way through to the outside. Seikei heard the clash of steel blades and understood this would be a fight to the death.

"Stay here," Reigen said. "Watch for the emperor. If you see him, take him to safety." He rode off toward the battle.

Seikei yearned to follow him, but Reigen was right. The important thing was to save the emperor—and Hato. Seikei scanned the mobs of people running away from the castle. There was no reason to expect them to be together, for Hato might never have been able to get near the emperor.

Seikei found it difficult to keep his eyes off Reigen. The old man had caught Yabuta's men by surprise, for they didn't expect anyone to attack them from behind. Seikei saw Reigen raise his sword and strike down with it. Yabuta's men began to fall one by one, as easily—yes—as if they had been blades of grass.

Others, now aware of the danger, turned to face Reigen. Seikei saw three of them at once try to bring him down from his horse, but they fell to the ground, bloodied. It was difficult to see what Reigen did to fight them off. Seikei had seen expert sword fighters, but none compared to Reigen. It was hard to believe that anyone could wield a sword that swiftly and effectively.

Was it really just the sword that was so powerful? Seikei found himself wishing he had been the one to take the Kusanagi from its resting place, just to see . . .

He shook his head to chase the thought away. Reigen's involvement in the fighting had allowed Lord Ponzu's forces to break through the barricade. With a shout of triumph they poured through the portal, hacking at their remaining enemies.

Now that the entrance was open, a whole host of people followed the samurai through it. Servants, laborers, women of the household, even some children. On the back of his horse, Reigen remained above the fray, searching the faces in the crowd. Seikei rode closer to help him look for Risu and Hato.

Suddenly a young woman blocked his way by kneeling in front of his horse. Seikei had to pull the reins sharply to keep from trampling her. "Get out of the way!" he shouted.

She looked up at him, her hands pressed together. "Sire!" she cried. "Forgive me! I have a message for you!"

He leaned over and tried to speak so that only she could hear him. "What did you call me?"

"Oh, Sire, Hato said you would be angry, but she had a good reason for telling me . . . who you are."

Seikei didn't know whether to be annoyed with Hato

or relieved that she must still be alive. "How did you, um, recognize me?" he asked the woman.

"Hato said you would be wearing a delivery boy's jacket. I beg your pardon for mentioning it. And of course your hachimaki."

Seikei put his hand to his forehead. He had nearly forgotten the headband on which he had written the word *honor.*

"Very good," he said. "Now tell me the message."

"Hato said to tell you Lord Ponzu's men have taken Risu to the Suzuka Mountains and she went with them."

"They did?" he said. "When was this?"

"This morning, Sire. Before the fire."

"Where exactly in the mountains did they go?"

"I'm not sure. It was a place that Risu wanted to visit. I'm . . . I have to beg your pardon again, Sire."

"For what?"

"I suppose you're aware that Lord Ponzu thinks Risu is the emperor. Not that that's true," she added hastily.

"Yes, I understand. That's all right."

"Well, Risu seemed to want to visit some place that belongs to you."

"To me."

"Yes, Sire, but of course the servants would realize he wasn't you. They wouldn't allow him inside."

"I'm sure," said Seikei. He was getting impatient. He had to find Reigen and tell him this news.

"Hato said to tell you that she will try to have the servants take Risu prisoner. She'll keep him there till you arrive."

Seikei was barely listening. He was getting a headache from trying to keep straight who thought he was the emperor and who didn't. He couldn't see Reigen anymore. He must have gone inside the castle grounds. "You have done well," he told the young woman. "When I'm . . . back in Kyoto again, I will try and reward you."

She bowed low, and Seikei urged his horse forward. There were too many people fleeing the fire through this gate, however, and he made slow progress.

Without warning, someone yanked the reins from his hands. Seikei reached for his sword, but before he could draw it, a mounted rider on his other side grabbed his arm. Seikei felt the point of a knife on his neck.

"Do not resist," the man with the knife said. "We do not want to hurt you."

"What do you want, then?" Seikei asked.

"To bring you to someone who wishes to speak to you."

Seikei took a deep breath. Without Reigen, he could do nothing, and the old man was nowhere in sight.

Seikei dismounted and allowed the two men to lead him away.

They moved with the crowd fleeing the burning castle. The men took him into a side street that wound uphill. At the top, they came into an open square where there was an excellent view of the castle grounds. Taking full advantage of it was Yabuta.

21 — Lord Ponzu's Silence

"You might send your messages on paper," Seikei said. "That way, you wouldn't waste the time of so many of your men."

Yabuta glared at him. "I like to see that people *understand* my messages," he said. "Apparently there was some confusion about the last one. I wanted the sword, and you helped someone else steal it."

"I did exactly what you told me to do," said Seikei. "I did not know that another person would take it."

"You *came* here with the man who has it," said Yabuta. Evidently, he saw a lot from this hill. "Now he has used it against my samurai."

"I chose to serve him," said Seikei, "because he rescued me from Takanori."

Yabuta nodded, as if he knew this already. "I thought Takanori would not be able to hold you," he murmured. He shrugged. "He is no great loss."

The loss was yours, Seikei thought. Because he told me you urged Lord Ponzu to rebel against the shogun. That is a secret I'm sure you do not want to be known.

"But the sword . . . ," Yabuta said. "I regret that loss. I must have it. I want you to tell Reigen to give it to me."

Seikei could not conceal his surprise. "How do you know his name?"

"Even from here I recognized him," said Yabuta. "It has not been that long since he left Kyoto. Supposedly he was in retirement, but he does not seem to be a man who has taken up a life of contemplation."

"He was forced to take the sword because you sent me to get it."

"Yes?" One of Yabuta's eyebrows went up. "Well, I am sorry to put him to so much trouble. Because now I want him to give it to me."

"I am certain he will never do that," said Seikei.

"Are you? Then perhaps you won't mind delivering a message to him from me."

"What is it?"

"Tell Reigen that I have his grandson. And if he wishes Yasuhito to live, he must bring me the sword."

Seikei was thunderstruck. *Yasuhito? That was Risu's real name.* "Grandson? The emperor is Reigen's grandson?"

Yabuta smiled in an ugly manner. "Oh, so there *are* still things you do not know, in your infinite wisdom? Yes, Reigen is the retired emperor, Yasuhito's grandfather. Frankly, if you *didn't* know that, I don't understand why you chose to follow him."

"Because he is a man of honor," said Seikei.

"Let us hope you are right and he chooses to save his grandson."

Seikei thought rapidly. Yabuta must be lying. The servant who stopped Seikei had said that Risu had gone to the mountains with Lord Ponzu's men. Yabuta was bluffing, but at least it gave Seikei a chance to inform Reigen what was happening.

"I will take him the message," Seikei said.

"Good. And then, if I were you, I would go back to Edo immediately," said Yabuta. "That way, you can be the first to give the shogun the happy news that I have put down Lord Ponzu's rebellion."

"Have you?" asked Seikei skeptically.

"I would say so," Yabuta replied. He snapped his fingers at one of his men. "Show our young friend my trophy," he said.

The man disappeared behind a rock and returned carrying a leather basket. He held it out so that Seikei could look inside. Seikei blinked at the sight of a man's severed head, looking up at him through half-open eyes.

"This is Lord Ponzu," said Yabuta. "I'd say his rebellion is over, wouldn't you?"

Yes, thought Seikei. And he can no longer tell anyone who encouraged him to plan that rebellion.

Seikei made his way down the hill and back to the castle. It was clear that the rebellion, if there had been one, was over. The castle was still burning, but now most of the people had either escaped it or died trying to do so.

No one stopped Seikei as he entered the gate that Reigen had fought his way through. He followed a trail of bodies. It seemed that the samurai of both sides had tried to stop Reigen. He had dealt with them all alike.

Of course, Seikei thought bitterly, how could one think of anyone in this affair as having loyalty to one side or the other? There was so much treachery that he wondered if anyone knew what *honor* meant.

He came upon a little stone garden that had been constructed as a place of beauty. Now it was ruined by people who had run through it in panic. A dead samurai lay facedown on the edge of the gravel bed. Reigen sat next to him, eyes closed, in a position of meditation.

As soon as Seikei's foot moved a pebble, Reigen's hand went to the hilt of his sword. He looked up, sadness in his eyes. "I have not been able to find Yasuhito," he said. "I sense he is no longer here. Have you come to tell me he is dead?"

"Not dead, but I fear he is in great danger," Seikei said.

"Sit here and tell me what you know."

Seikei hesitated. "I cannot sit with you as if we were equals," he said. "I know who you are."

Reigen frowned. "You mean . . . that I was once the emperor."

Seikei bowed his head.

"Listen to me," said Reigen. "We have the same goal, do we not?"

"To save the emperor," agreed Seikei. And Hato, he thought.

"Then we must do whatever is necessary to achieve that goal."

"As long as it is honorable."

"That goes without saying. It is honorable for you to

treat me as your equal—even as your servant—if that will help us reach our goal. Do you agree?"

"Yes, I understand that," Seikei said.

"Good. Now sit and tell me what you have learned."

After Seikei described his meeting with the servant, Reigen nodded. "I know the place she means. When Yasuhito was a small boy, we had a lodge in the mountains. During the summer, when Kyoto became too warm, we would go there. There were only a few of us—perhaps fifty to sixty servants, his parents, and I. But he may not know that the place was shut up after his father died. It will be deserted now."

Reigen rose and brushed himself off. "We will start at once," he said. He stopped when he saw Seikei's face. "Have you anything else to tell me?" he asked.

Seikei was worried. "I should have told you this first. Yabuta is here." He repeated the message Yabuta had wanted him to deliver.

"And you believe Yabuta can see us now?" Reigen asked.

Seikei indicated the hilltop where he had met Yabuta. It was possible to make out the group of samurai who were still standing there.

"But Yabuta *couldn't* have the emperor," Seikei said. "The servant told me he was taken away by Lord Ponzu's men."

"Do not forget that some of Ponzu's samurai were actually working for Yabuta," Reigen said.

Seikei had to admit this was true. "But you . . . you mustn't . . ." He bit his lip. It was not his place to tell an emperor what his duty was. Then Seikei saw the joke in this, and smiled. That was exactly what his original mission had been.

"I believe," said Reigen, "that we must reach the emperor before Yabuta does."

"But Yabuta will follow us if you do not give him the sword," said Seikei.

"He can try," Reigen replied. "Are you willing to travel with me wherever I go?"

Seikei had no doubts. "I will," he said.

"And you have not forgotten your promise? To use *your* sword when it is time?"

Seikei hesitated before answering. "I have not forgotten," he said. But silently he wondered if he could really use his sword to attack Reigen. And even if he *did*—how could Reigen be defeated?

"More than ever, that is important," Reigen said. "The

Kusanagi must be returned to its resting place. Swear that you will do it."

"I swear."

"Then let us go swiftly where Yabuta and his men cannot follow us," Reigen said.

Seikei was going to ask where that could be, but it was unnecessary. Reigen had already turned and was striding straight toward the still-burning castle.

22 – Acting Like Fish

Seikei had to hurry to catch up with Reigen. He had many questions to ask. The most important of them was whether Reigen realized they would be burned alive.

Fortunately the flames had not yet reached this part of the castle, although they soon would. Smoke filled the great hallway at the entrance, and Reigen told Seikei to bend low as he walked. It was easier to breathe near the floor.

Seikei could not understand what Reigen was doing here. Even if they passed through the castle and came out another door, Yabuta would still be able to see them from his vantage point. In fact, since Yabuta must have realized that Reigen had no intention of giving up the sword, he might have his men surrounding the castle right now.

Reigen took a left turn into a short corridor. When Seikei followed, he nearly panicked, for it looked as if the old man had disappeared. Then he saw a flight of stairs headed down into what looked like a pit of black ink. Seikei set his foot on the staircase and heard Reigen headed farther down. There was nothing to do but go after him.

The air here was not as smoky. In fact, Seikei could feel a damp breeze coming from the bottom of the pit. That seemed impossible, for there could be no windows down here.

To steady himself, Seikei put his hand out to the side and felt a stone wall. Perhaps it was Reigen's plan to hide in some forgotten dungeon until Yabuta gave up looking for them. No, that was not like Reigen. He must want to find his grandson as swiftly as possible.

"Stop here." Reigen's voice was right in front of Seikei, who would have run into the old emperor if he hadn't spoken. The silence here was so complete that Seikei could hear himself breathing. Maybe that was only because he was panting from trying to keep up with Reigen.

Then he became aware of another sound, very faint but continuous. Seikei held his breath so he could hear it better.

Water. Flowing water.

"Can you swim?" asked Reigen.

"A little," Seikei said. He wasn't sure he could swim in total darkness without having any idea where he was going.

"You may not have to," said Reigen. "This is a tunnel that brings fresh water to the castle. In the spring, when snow melts in the mountains, the stream can be deep. Right now, it is probably shallow enough so that we will only get our feet wet. Take off your sandals and tabi."

Seikei did so, following Reigen into the water. It was not cold, but on the bottom were sharp rocks that hurt his feet. Worse than that was when he stepped on something soft and slimy, and it wriggled away. To his shame, Seikei cried out in surprise.

"There are snakes in the water," Reigen told him, "frogs, slugs, and other creatures. But few of them are poisonous."

Seikei prayed he wouldn't step on any more. There was no way for him to tread carefully, because Reigen kept moving ahead at a rapid pace. Once, Seikei's foot slipped and he fell to one knee. He got up again and had to move even faster. He had no idea how far they had walked, but it seemed to him as if they must have gone well beyond the limits of the castle grounds.

Finally he realized he could dimly see the water, and then the walls of the tunnel as well. They were nearing daylight again. Rounding a bend, Seikei caught a glimpse of the sky.

They emerged at a place where the stream met the Shonai River. Seikei looked back. The hill beyond the castle was obscured by smoke. He could no longer see anyone up there, which must mean Yabuta couldn't see them either.

Or could he? Seikei had learned not to underestimate the spy chief. Truly it seemed as if his eyes were everywhere. When he saw Reigen and Seikei enter the castle, he must have known there was another way out. Perhaps even now he had moved to another vantage point and was looking down at them.

Seikei shivered. A chilly wind was blowing up from Ise Bay. Reigen turned in that direction, walking along the riverbank. At least there were other people here—some fishing, some washing clothes. Brightly colored rectangles were laid out on the ground, for people brought freshly dyed cloth here to rinse in the water.

With all the activity, Reigen and Seikei would not be so easy to spot from a distance.

A man with a small rowboat asked if they wished to cross the river. "I charge two ryo per person," he said, "but for you and your grandson, only three ryo."

"I would rather have the boat," said Reigen.

The man did not quite understand. "You do not need the boat," he said. "I will take you across."

"How much do you want for the boat?" Reigen persisted.

The man shook his head. "If you take my boat, I have no way to earn a living."

"You can buy another boat," Reigen said. "But we need this one now."

The man looked at Reigen the way he would have regarded a crazy person. He wanted to laugh, but he also wanted to get away from him.

"Tell you what," the man said, smiling, trying to humor Reigen. "You can have the boat for an *oban*."

"Fine," said Reigen. He drew a small bag from his kimono and took out an oval gold coin.

The boatman's eyes widened. He put out his hand for the coin, and Seikei saw that it was trembling. But when Reigen gave him the oban, the man seemed to weigh it suspiciously. No doubt, thought Seikei, he had never held an oban before. It did not weigh as much as the copper coins he saw every day. Cautiously, he put the edge of it in his mouth and bit down hard. If the coin was really gold, he knew, his teeth would make an impression. He examined it. Finding teeth marks, he slowly nodded and moved aside, indicating that the boat was now theirs.

Reigen stepped into the boat and motioned to Seikei, who promptly pushed it off the sandy beach and scrambled inside.

"I will row from here," said Reigen. "Since the river flows into the bay, it will be little work."

Seikei looked back to see the boatman standing on the river's edge, still staring at them. "You didn't have to give him an oban," said Seikei.

"He asked for an oban," Reigen replied. "I did not wish to waste time arguing."

"He would have been happy with less," said Seikei.

"If he is the type of person who is happy," said Reigen, "he will still be happy tomorrow. If he is the type of person who is unhappy, he will realize I might have given him *two* oban."

Seikei smiled.

"What he will probably *not* realize," continued Reigen, "is that if he had refused to sell me the boat, I would have killed him."

Seikei didn't smile at that, for it seemed Reigen was serious.

"That is the sort of thing that comes into your mind when you carry the Kusanagi," said Reigen. "That is why I do not want to hold it any longer than I have to."

"Where are we going?" Seikei asked after a moment.

"To the imperial lodge in the Suzuka Mountains."

"But we cannot get there in a boat."

"I hope Yabuta thinks that as well. I would imagine he has men waiting for us at the checkpoint on the Tokaido Road. Anyone leaving Nagoya in that direction would have to pass through there."

But you didn't, thought Seikei, remembering that Reigen had left the road to avoid the guards on the way in.

"See," Reigen said, pointing. "We are nearly at Ise Bay. The cormorant fishers are out."

True enough. At the point where the river flowed into the great bay, men were using cormorants to catch fish. They tied long cords around the necks of the birds, who resembled large ducks with hooked bills. The birds, as they would naturally, soared over the water looking for fish near the surface. When they spotted one, they dove swiftly, trying to scoop it into their beaks. Sometimes they disappeared entirely beneath the water in pursuit of their prey. If they were successful, their owners would reel in the cord and take the fish.

"It seems unfair," said Seikei, "that the birds do all the work and the man gets the reward. Is it true that they cannot swallow the fish because of the cord around their necks?"

"Yes," said Reigen, "but in the end they will receive a share of the catch. I find it interesting, however, that although many people feel sympathy for the birds, no one ever pities the fish."

Seikei smiled at the thought. "It's because fish are . . . well, there are just so many of them."

"And you cannot tell one fish from another," Reigen pointed out. "That is what we must be like now."

"Like the fish?"

"Just so," Reigen said. "Only we must swim very deep, so that Yabuta cannot see us."

Seikei half expected Reigen to order him to jump overboard and swim. After what had happened since Seikei left Edo, nothing would have surprised him. Or so he thought.

But that was not what the ex-emperor had in mind.

When they entered the bay, Reigen guided the boat along the shoreline to their right. It looked no different from any of the countless other small craft that dotted the bay. Anyone seeing Seikei and Reigen would think they were a grandson and grandfather out fishing.

Seikei still could not understand where they were going. Reigen continually scanned the shoreline, looking for something. But what? Seikei followed the old man's gaze, but saw nothing out of the ordinary: small villages, docks where boats were tied up, and, higher up the hills, rice paddies, tea plants, and household gardens.

"There is the place," Reigen said suddenly, and turned the boat sharply. He headed for the mouth of a small river, one of several that emptied into the bay.

"Your turn to row," said Reigen when they reached it. "We will need strong young arms to take us upstream."

"How far do we have to go?" asked Seikei.

"There," Reigen said, pointing.

Seikei turned to look and saw the mountains that lay in the distance. They seemed impossibly far. "Are you sure?" he asked.

"When I was a boy," said Reigen, "I came down this

river from the imperial lodge. Now we must go up to take the emperor from those who have him."

Well, thought Seikei, one thing is certain: Yabuta would never imagine we would travel this way. Nevertheless, as the boat headed up the river, he looked back to see if anyone was following them.

23 — The Kusanagi Speaks

Seikei woke up, still exhausted. His arms ached and his hands were on fire with blisters—not surprisingly, for he had rowed for a day and part of the previous night. All the time, he had been feeling more and more resentful. The thought had popped into his head that Risu was to blame for all this trouble. It would never have happened if Risu hadn't decided that he wasn't the emperor. And if he doesn't want to be emperor, thought Seikei, then find someone who does. Reigen was the sort of person who *ought* to be emperor. Even though Seikei remembered the judge saying Reigen couldn't resume his duties once he retired, certainly an exception ought to be made in this case.

All of those were unworthy thoughts, and Seikei knew better than to say them aloud to Reigen. Being angry had only one advantage: It gave Seikei the energy to keep rowing.

They had arrived at this spot after darkness had fallen. To Seikei it looked no different than virtually any other place they'd passed in the last day and a half. But once again, it had a special meaning for Reigen. He had guided Seikei to a place where the river ran beside a high cliff. Seikei feared the small wooden boat would be broken to pieces on the rocky face of the cliff. Just as they reached it, however, Reigen leaned over the side of the boat and pulled aside some shrubbery growing from a crack in the rock.

Behind it was a cave, just large enough for the boat to slide into. When the shrubbery snapped back into place, they were hidden from view. It was not comfortable sleeping in the bottom of the boat, but Seikei was so exhausted that he had not stayed awake for long.

Now, through the green shrubbery at the mouth of the cave, he could see sunlight. Seikei remembered the story of Amaterasu hiding in a cave until the other kami lured her out. He looked at Reigen, who was already awake. He was like Bunzo in that he never seemed to let down his guard. "I didn't get to ask you," said Seikei. "Why did you take the mirror from the imperial palace?"

"I will need it when we find the emperor," said Reigen. "Let us accomplish that before we correct other mistakes."

Seikei wondered if he was responsible for any of the "other mistakes." He hoped not, for he suspected Reigen's methods of correcting them would not be pleasant.

Slowly they edged the boat through the shrubbery again. Seikei saw what he had not been able to in the darkness the night before. Not far away was a dock. Beside it was a shelter where one could sit and admire the view. Beyond that was a stone path that led over a hill. At one time, it was clear that the grass and flowers at this spot had been carefully tended. Now, however, the path was overgrown. Where autumn leaves had fallen, no one had swept them up. It looked indeed as if the place had long been deserted.

Seikei rowed the boat to the dock and tied it up. Reigen stepped out, looking as if he were using all his senses to determine if anyone else was nearby. He motioned to Seikei, and said, "Stay in the boat. We may need to leave in a hurry."

Reigen took a few steps up the stone path. Without warning, a samurai appeared just at the top of the hill. He wore a kosode with Lord Ponzu's crest on it. The man seemed surprised to see anyone here. As well he might be, thought Seikei. No one else would have arrived by water.

"Who are you? What are you doing here?" the samurai called.

Reigen replied in a soft voice, "We are travelers looking for a place to stay." He started walking toward the samurai, his hands extended as if to show peaceful intent.

The samurai was angry. He drew his short sword and waved it in Reigen's direction. "Get out of here! At once!" he shouted.

Reigen kept walking toward him as though he were unable to understand. Seikei, watching, held his breath, for he fully understood the danger the samurai was in.

Reigen's refusal to obey made the samurai lose all sense of caution. He rushed forward, looking as if he intended to use his sword. The instant he was within striking distance, Reigen drew his own blade. Faster than Seikei's eyes could follow, he struck off the samurai's hand. It fell to the ground, still grasping the sword.

The samurai realized too late that he should not have come so close to the harmless-looking old man. He opened his mouth as if to call for help, but a second swipe of the Kusanagi silenced him for good.

Now Reigen turned and beckoned for Seikei to follow. Seikei obeyed, hoping more than ever that he would not have to keep his promise to Reigen. As he passed the samurai's lifeless body, Seikei glanced down and reflected that this would be his own fate should he ever dare to use his wooden sword against the ex-emperor.

At the top of the hill, they looked down on a beautiful scene. In a glade below was a rustic building that might have been the cottage of a humble mountain family, except for its vast size. The upward-curving wooden eaves had been left unpainted and the roof tiles selected to look as if they were stones randomly picked up in the woods.

It still seemed deserted, but Seikei knew that was an illusion. Somewhere inside the lodge was the emperor. And Hato. He sniffed the air, but detected no scent of ginkgo porridge. That was a bad sign, he thought. Perhaps someone had already killed both Risu and Hato.

Reigen walked briskly now, with no attempt to conceal his approach. Three samurai emerged from the house and stood on the porch. They did not look as fearless as the first one, although like him, they wore the crest of Lord Ponzu.

Reigen stopped and called to them, "What are you doing in my house?"

"Your house?" one of them replied. "This isn't your house. This is the emperor's house."

"Don't you recognize me?" Reigen shouted. He put his hand on the hilt of his sword.

The three samurai spoke among themselves. "The emperor is inside," one of them said.

"I am his grandfather," Reigen replied. "And this is the Kusanagi." He raised the sword from its scabbard and held it high. "Do you dare to stand in my way?" he called to the samurai.

One of them apparently did. He unsheathed his own sword and looked at his companions for support. They hesitated.

That didn't stop the bold samurai. "He's just an old man," he said, jumping down from the porch and assuming a fighting position in front of Reigen.

As Reigen's arm came down, the samurai tried to block the sword with his own. Seikei approved of the tactic, which would have worked had the two been equally matched. But the Kusanagi could not be thwarted. It shattered the samurai's sword as easily as if it had been made of plaster. Reigen's blow continued downward and the Kusanagi sliced through the samurai's arm at the elbow. Blood gushed from the wound and the man fell to his knees. He tried helplessly to stanch the bleeding and then fainted.

Reigen didn't give him a second glance. "Well?" he called to the other two.

They didn't need to confer to reach a decision. They

ran to the end of the porch, jumped, and soon vanished into a grove of trees.

"They have no honor," Seikei commented.

"They serve their master for gain, not for honor," replied Reigen. "Which do you value more, life or honor?"

"Honor," replied Seikei dutifully, "because everyone must die, but honor lasts forever."

"Remember your promise, then," Reigen said, starting up the steps of the lodge.

Grasping the hilt of his sword to hide his nervousness, Seikei followed. The front door led into a hallway that contained a wall shrine to Amaterasu. A candleholder beneath it held only scraps of wax. Three corridors led into other parts of the lodge.

Reigen motioned for Seikei to be silent. The lodge seemed absolutely still. It was as if no one had been there for years. But Reigen seemed to notice something. He cocked his head and then chose one of the corridors.

Trailing him, Seikei could see that a door stood open at the other end of the hallway. Reigen stepped through the entrance and stopped. Seikei, standing behind him, saw that Yabuta had arrived before them after all.

"I've been waiting for you," the spy chief said. "And

since you have defeated my guards, I know that you have brought me what I want." He looked at Seikei with his cold eyes. "Thank you for delivering my message."

Seikei's heart sank. Yabuta was seated on a mat, holding a knife to the throat of the boy emperor. Risu—or Yasuhito, as his proper name was—had his hands tied behind his back. His face wore an expression Seikei had not see there before: terror.

"I *told* him he had the wrong person, but he wouldn't believe me." Hato's voice came from another part of the room. She too had her hands tied. Seikei could not help but wonder why Yabuta had not gagged her as well.

"This girl," said Yabuta, "has the odd idea that the boy I hold is not the emperor. Apparently, Judge Ooka's stepson had been practicing his impersonation even before I suggested it to him. Is that so?"

"There was a misunderstanding," Seikei said.

"Well, let us clear it up at once, shall we? If I am not holding the real emperor, then his grandfather may of course use his sword to kill me. But if this boy is in fact Yasuhito, his grandfather will not want to see his throat slit. And make no mistake, my hand will move faster than he can reach me. Do you wish to see your grandson die?" he called to Reigen.

"No," Reigen said in a low voice.

"Then remove the Kusanagi—in its scabbard, if you please—and lay it on the floor in front of me."

Reigen began to untie the scabbard from the obi around his waist.

"No!" cried Seikei. "You can't!"

"I must," Reigen said. "You heard him."

"But Yabuta will use the sword to make himself the ruler of Japan."

"Only a descendant of Amaterasu can be the ruler," said Reigen. "Yabuta can be a shogun, but no matter who is shogun, the emperor reigns."

Reigen freed the scabbard that contained the Kusanagi. Holding it in both hands, as if making an offering, he stepped forward and laid it in front of Yabuta.

When Reigen stepped back, Yabuta shoved Yasuhito away and snatched up the sword. Pulling it from its scabbard, he admired it as keenly as if he were seeing his own image in the shining steel.

Then his eyes, glittering with triumph, slowly turned in Seikei's direction.

24 – Yasuhito Sees

"Now is the time," said Reigen.

Seikei wasn't sure, at first, what he was talking about. Then it came to him.

Now? Well, of course he was going to die anyway, so why not? Better to die defending one's honor than whimpering for mercy.

Seikei drew the wooden sword from his obi.

When Yabuta saw that, he laughed. It sounded like the cawing of a crow that has found a great hoard of spilled rice.

"So your arrogant pride persists?" Yabuta said. "I will enjoy stopping it once and for all." He leaped forward, preparing to cut Seikei in two with the Kusanagi.

Seikei had been trained in the art of the sword by Bunzo and the actor Tomomi. He had also seen the ninja master Tatsuno use a sword, and gained much knowledge from that. Seikei's only advantage in this fight was that Yabuta expected him to be completely inexperienced.

Thus, when Yabuta brought the deadly blade down, Seikei was no longer there. After seeing Yabuta commit himself, Seikei had sidestepped the blade.

That gave him a chance to strike at Yabuta. Seikei's maple sword whipped through the air, but unfortunately only gave the spy chief a glancing blow on his shoulder.

Even that was enough to enrage Yabuta. He swung full force at Seikei, this time using a side-to-side blow. Seikei ducked under it much the same way he had seen Tatsuno do. Seikei retaliated with a thrust aimed at Yabuta's face. He had hoped to strike an eye, but hit Yabuta's nose instead. Satisfyingly, to Seikei, it started to bleed.

He expected Yabuta to become more reckless after that, but the spy chief was no fool. He controlled his anger and began to stalk Seikei. Step by step Seikei moved back, trying to stay out of reach of the razor-sharp Kusanagi that Yabuta swung back and forth in front of him. Finally Seikei was forced against a wall. Yabuta feinted with the point of his sword, and Seikei dodged to one side. This time, Yabuta anticipated the move and he slashed in the same direction.

Seikei brought up his wooden sword, the only thing

he could do to defend himself. Of course if the edge of the Kusanagi had struck it, the wood would have split as easily as a piece of straw. Luckily, Seikei's sword caught the flat of the blade, diverting it just enough so that Seikei could slip away.

Trying to gain more space in which to maneuver, Seikei turned his back and ran. The trouble with this tactic was that if Seikei weren't quick enough, he would be defenseless against an attack. Yabuta's footsteps sounded uncomfortably near.

Then Seikei heard a crash and a curse from Yabuta. He turned and saw the spy chief on the floor. Hato had stuck out her leg and tripped him.

Yabuta was down only for an instant. He jumped to his feet and seemed about to slash at Hato. Seikei instinctively struck downward with the wooden sword. He aimed at the back of Yabuta's head, but the spy chief realized the blow was coming and ducked under it.

Yabuta turned, his eyes blazing hatred at Seikei. He took two more sideways swipes, which Seikei easily evaded. Seikei realized the man was breathing hard and carried the Kusanagi as if it were too heavy for him. That was odd, for Yabuta was much younger than Reigen, who had used the sword with ease.

Trying to see if he could use Yabuta's weakness to his

advantage, Seikei gave up trying to parry his opponent's blows. Instead, he merely dodged them, nimbly hopping, ducking, or darting aside whenever Yabuta tried to strike him.

It was a risky strategy, but it seemed to be working: With each blow, Yabuta appeared to grow more exhausted. In fact, it became obvious that Seikei could continue to evade him almost indefinitely. Finally, Yabuta stood, barely holding the sword off the floor, his agonized breaths loud enough for everyone to hear.

"Now is the time," Reigen said again.

Yes, Seikei thought. Now I have the advantage.

He slid forward without lifting his feet, raising his sword as he moved. Yabuta saw the blow coming and tried to lift the Kusanagi to block it. But he failed. Seikei hit him soundly across the side of the head, with a ferocity that he had not known he felt. The blow made a noise like a branch snapping off a tree.

Yabuta fell to the floor and lay there motionless.

"Did you kill him?" Hato called out. "If not, hit him again."

Seikei looked down. He realized that he was trembling from the fight. He could not bring himself to speak.

Reigen came and crouched over Yabuta's body. "He is

alive," he said. "He does not deserve to die so easily." He rose and looked at Seikei. "Take the sword," he said.

Seikei looked, without comprehending, at the wooden sword he still held.

"The Kusanagi," Reigen urged again. "Take it."

Seikei bent and pried the sword from Yabuta's grasp. It was, indeed, heavier than he would have guessed. He gave Reigen a questioning glance. "Do you want it?" Seikei asked.

"No," said Reigen. "You must return it to the Atsuta Shrine. Will you do that?"

"Yes," Seikei said.

"It is not for you to use," said Reigen.

"Was that why . . . Yabuta grew so tired?" Seikei asked.

Reigen nodded. "Only a descendant of Amaterasu may use it. The kami of the sword began to fight Yabuta."

"Grandfather," came another voice. They turned to look at Yasuhito, crouched in a corner of the room. "*I* want the Kusanagi," he said. "Don't give it to him."

"You have no need for the Kusanagi, Yasuhito," said Reigen.

"But I *do.* When I read—" He looked around. "I don't want to say, with them here."

"They are loyal to you," said Reigen. "You can trust them."

Yasuhito looked at Hato. "Well, she makes good porridge, anyway," he said. "But what about him?" he added, pointing to Seikei.

"He has already read the Kusanagi scroll, if that's what you're worried about," said Reigen.

"Oh, he did?" Yasuhito seemed surprised.

"You told me to look for it, remember?" said Seikei.

"I guess I did. Anyway, the scroll said that the *real* sword was at the Atsuta Shrine, not in the imperial palace. The one in the palace is only a copy."

"That is true," said Reigen. "When Prince Yamato placed the sword at Atsuta, he intended that it would never be used again. So a copy was made to be used in the ceremony when a new emperor comes to the throne."

"But I thought because the sword that they gave me at my . . . the ceremony when I became emperor . . . wasn't real, that was the *reason*."

"The reason for what?"

Yasuhito looked as if he were fighting back tears. In spite of everything, Seikei felt sorry for him. "The reason why Amaterasu didn't come to see me during the night I spent in the hut at the ceremony. I waited and waited, because I was going to ask her where *you* had gone. But she never came. I didn't fall asleep either, the way Uino said I must have. So that meant . . . that meant I wasn't really the emperor. Of course, Uino made me act like I was, but then he died this year and I decided I wasn't going to do it anymore."

Seikei stared at Yasuhito. He wondered how the judge would react when he heard about this. "But you mustn't—" Seikei started to say. Then he felt Reigen's hand on his arm.

"This," the old man said, "is something I will take care of. But not here. This room is unclean now. Untie Hato and let me have the cord."

Seikei obeyed.

"Now take the others into the garden outside the lodge," Reigen said. "I will see that Yabuta does no more harm."

The three young people left the lodge and found a stone garden that badly needed raking and cleaning. "Whenever I thought of this place, I remembered this garden," Yasuhito said. "My mother would hold me on her lap and tell me stories. It was the last time I was happy."

Hato gave Seikei a look. "Tell him who you really are," she said. "I'm tired of keeping your secret."

"Keeping my secret?" said Seikei. "What about the servant you sent to find me at Ponzu's castle?"

"Well, I had to tell *her,*" said Hato. "And it worked out all right. You found us, didn't you?"

Seikei had no answer for this. Which was just as well, for Reigen emerged from the house just then.

"You must kneel," he told Seikei and Hato. Seikei did so at once, but Hato was indignant and had to be coaxed.

Then Reigen stood facing Yasuhito. "Grandson," he said, "tell me about the night you spent in the hut at the ceremony when you were raised to the throne. When sunrise came, did you look in the mirror that is one of the three treasures of Amaterasu?"

"The mirror? No, Grandfather, I was upset because I thought Amaterasu had failed to come visit me."

Reigen looked at the sky. Seikei followed his gaze. It was a clear, crisp day and the sun was almost overhead. It was so bright that it was impossible for Seikei to keep his eyes raised for long.

When he looked down, he saw Reigen take a flat, shining object from his kimono. "Here," he said to Yasuhito, "here is what you should have seen." He tilted the sacred mirror until it reflected the rays of the sun directly into Yasuhito's face.

Yasuhito, who should have blinked, instead stared intently into the light. He reached forward to touch the mirror. "Grandfather!" he said. "I see her! She looks . . . like me."

"So she should," said Reigen. "For you are her true descendant."

Having waited so long, Yasuhito seemed unable to take his eyes from what he saw in the mirror. Seikei watched the boy's face. It changed—became more like Reigen's, even though they were far apart in age. Before this, Yasuhito had seemed like just another boy, and not one Seikei would care to know well. Now it was clear who he was.

When the ceremony was over, Reigen said to Seikei and Hato, "You may come and bow to the emperor."

Seikei did so, and felt it was an honor he would always remember. He took off his headband and laid it before the emperor. His task was accomplished.

But Hato approached reluctantly. "I want to understand something," she said. Pointing to Yasuhito, she said, "You really *are* the emperor?"

Yasuhito nodded. "Grandfather has made me understand my error."

"Hmph," she sniffed. "I wouldn't think it was something you could be in any doubt about." She turned her attention to Reigen. "And if you're his grandfather, then you *used* to be the emperor."

"That is so," Reigen responded. "When you asked me earlier if I was a kami, I could not truthfully answer no, because even though I am no longer emperor, I still carry the spirit of Amaterasu within me."

Hato finally turned to Seikei. She looked dismayed. "So you're the only one who *wasn't* the emperor?" she asked.

"I'm sorry," said Seikei. "I tried to tell you, but there was so much confusion . . ." He trailed off.

Hato thought about it for a moment, then made her decision. "I think you're still all trying to trick me," she said.

25 – Seikei's Only Mistake

It was a fine spring day, when the sun seemed to chase away the cold air that had hung over the earth all winter. Seikei and the judge stood in the gardens outside the imperial palace, waiting for the plowing ceremony to begin. The judge was there as the shogun's official representative, and Seikei had received a personal invitation. He noticed that it had been signed by both the Ministers of the Right and of the Left. He wondered how they could have been persuaded to do such a thing together. If they realized who he was, they would probably not have sent it at all.

In fact, Seikei had not really wanted to come. The entire affair had involved so much treachery that he didn't want to revisit the scene. The judge, however, had told Seikei that no one could refuse an invitation from the imperial court.

Months ago, when Seikei had returned to Edo and

made his report, the shogun had been greatly disturbed. He pointed out that Seikei really had no proof that Yabuta had helped to plan the rebellion. "All you know," he told Seikei, "is what the ronin Takanori told you. He may have been lying, and now he is dead." The shogun sent samurai to find Yabuta, but they could not locate him anywhere.

Seikei recalled the last time he had seen the spy chief, in the imperial lodge in the mountains. Reigen had sent the others out of the room and said he would make sure Yabuta did no more harm.

There was no way to ask Reigen what he had done, because after returning the emperor to the palace, he had disappeared again. Seikei had been busy returning the Kusanagi to its place in the shrine and had no chance to say good-bye. At the shrine, the priests still thought Seikei was the emperor, making it easier for him to return the sword without explaining where it had been.

"The shogun knows you did a good job," the judge assured Seikei. "After all, the spring plowing ceremony will take place as scheduled. The shogun is only upset because he has to find a new chief for the Guards of the Inner Garden."

"He should not *have* a chief to do that kind of work," said Seikei.

"I am afraid that rulers always like to know what their subjects are up to," said the judge.

A murmur went through the crowd of invited guests. Two stable hands led a water buffalo into the garden and began to hitch it to a plow. Seikei looked at the animal with some doubt. "I hope the emperor can handle such a huge beast," he said.

"It was carefully chosen for its gentleness," the judge murmured. "The ground to be plowed has been loosened beforehand and all stones removed. I don't think the work will strain the emperor's abilities."

A priest rang a handbell, the signal for everyone to kneel. A moment later, the emperor appeared, with a minister on each side of him. The two officials were whispering in both his ears at once. Seikei was pretty sure their advice was worthless.

Finally the emperor stepped forward, and a priest handed him the reins and a whip. The whip was unnecessary. As soon as the emperor jiggled the reins, the water buffalo took exactly six steps forward and then stopped. The animal was as well trained as the emperor—perhaps better.

At any rate, a satisfactory furrow had now been cut into the ground. The emperor took some seeds from one of the priests and dropped them in, spaced equally apart.

Now another priest handed him a small spade, sparkling clean. Yasuhito used it to cover the seeds. Seikei knew that once the seeds sprouted, they would be transplanted into a water-filled paddy, where they could grow till the harvest. The emperor would have other roles to fill then, but for today, he had done his job perfectly.

The emperor knew it. Seikei thought he saw a smile pass over Yasuhito's face as he stepped back from the furrow. And when the two ministers closed in to whisper additional instructions to him, he pushed them away. Not roughly—maybe no one but Seikei noticed it—but a very definite push. He knew he was emperor now.

The guests bowed deeply as the emperor left the garden, and then got to their feet. In a little while, they would enter the palace for a banquet.

Seikei saw Hato threading her way through the crowd. She wore the uniform of a palace servant. Seikei steeled himself, not knowing what she might say.

But all she wanted was to ask if they were staying for the banquet. "I made the porridge," she said. "The emperor won't allow anyone but me to make it. Sometimes his personal servants wake me up at night to make it."

"So you finally accepted the fact that he is the emperor?" said Seikei.

She nodded. "Well, he's given me a good job, so I follow orders." She looked around to see if anybody was listening. Fortunately the judge was talking to another guest.

"But you would have made a better emperor," Hato said with a wink. She disappeared into the crowd before Seikei could say anything.

Later, when the porridge was served, Seikei tasted a spoonful. No doubt about it: Hato was a great cook, at least if you liked ginkgo porridge. He ate some more.

The judge finished his own bowl and turned to Seikei. "You should be proud," he said. "The success of this day is due to your efforts."

"I had a lot of help," Seikei said modestly.

"But I now have a criticism to offer."

Seikei cringed. He knew there were many things he had done wrong, but he had corrected most of them. He had even managed to redeem his swords from the pawnbroker. Would the judge think it had been too disrespectful for him to pawn them in the first place?

"That young woman who spoke to you in the garden," said the judge, showing once again that he missed nothing. "Was she the one who thought that you were the emperor?"

Seikei nodded. "I know it was wrong of me to let her think that, but—"

"And she made this porridge?" the Judge asked.

"Yes. That was what she came to tell me."

"You should never have let her get away. I wish you had brought her home with you. She's much too good to be cooking for the emperor."

Authors' Note

The Japanese claim their nation has the longest continuous line of rulers in the world. The first emperor, according to tradition, was Jimmu, who reigned from 660 B.C. to 585 B.C., by the modern calendar. Official historians have listed each of the 126 emperors, down to the current one, Akihito, who was enthroned in 1989. Japanese emperors are not "crowned," because the headgear they wear is not a crown.

Japanese emperors are known by one name when they are alive, but another name is applied to them and their reign after they have left the throne. Thus, most Americans knew the 125th emperor by the name Hirohito, but after his death his reign name became Showa.

The young emperor in our story, Yasuhito, ruled Japan in the early 1700s, coming to the throne at the age of eight. His grandfather Reigen had reigned from 1663 to 1687, when he retired. Reigen lived on for another forty-five years. Yasuhito's reign name is Nakamikado, which is how you will find him on a list of Japanese emperors. All the events in our story concerning these two emperors are completely from the imaginations of the authors.

The story of Amaterasu and Susanoo is part of Japanese mythology. Prince Yamato, who used the Kusanagi to conquer rebellious tribes, is supposed to have lived around A.D. 100. His formal name is Yamato-Dake, or Yamato the Warlike. The Kusanagi is still in the Atsuta Shrine at Nagoya today. However, though you may visit the shrine, the sword is never displayed to the public.

There really were pawnbrokers, known as *tamamakiya,* in Japan in the 1700s. The Mitsui family, whose name can still be found on Japanese banks, insurance companies, and real estate interests, began as pawnbrokers in the early 1600s.

We have simplified our description of the ceremonies at which a new emperor is enthroned. He does, however, spend a night in a hut waiting for his ancestor Amaterasu to visit. What happens during that night is known only to the emperor.

As readers of *The Ghost in the Tokaido Inn, The Demon in the Teahouse,* and *In Darkness, Death* know, Judge Ooka was a real person whose reputation for wise and honest decisions won him promotion to high office. He served Yoshimune, the eighth shogun of the Tokugawa family, who ruled Japan between 1717 and 1744. Tales about Judge Ooka have remained popular, causing some to call him the Sherlock Holmes of Japan. The character of his stepson, Seikei, is thc authors' creation.